A PONY called SECRET

A New Beginning

OLIVIA TUFFIN

For W.T. Always...

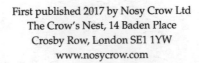

First published 2017 by Nosy Crow Ltd
The Crow's Nest, 14 Baden Place
Crosby Row, London SE1 1YW
www.nosycrow.com

ISBN: 978 0 85763 952 3

Text © Olivia Tuffin 2017
Pony photographs © Matthew Bishop Photography 2017

The right of Olivia Tuffin to be identified as the author has been asserted.

A CIP catalogue record for this book is available from the British Library.

Printed and bound in the UK by Clays Ltd, St Ives Plc.
Typeset by Tiger Media

Papers used by Nosy Crow are made from wood grown in
sustainable forests.

8642

PROLOGUE

The Highland gelding was snow white in colour, and his thick mane fell perfectly, each and every tangle carefully combed out. "That's better," the boy smiled, giving the pony a pat. When he was with his horse the boy could forget everything, all of the heartbreak from the last year, all of the worry that lay ahead. Lost in thought, he gave a start as someone came into the stable next to him.

The man was on the phone and clearly unaware his every word could be heard. Keeping as still as possible, his pony's ears pricked up and the boy felt his blood run cold.

"She's got to be loaded. She inherited this place!" The man was laughing. "And yet she's putting everything into this stupid team. 'Oh, here come the Flying Fillies!'" he mocked. "But the ponies are top quality, and could be worth a lot in the right hands…"

There was a pause, then another peal of harsh laughter.

"Working on it." The man's voice was gleeful. "As soon as I persuade her to ditch this dump of a yard and her weird brother. Give me time…"

The stable door banged and the voice faded away. The boy could breathe again.

Placing a trembling hand on his pony's mane, the boy held his head up high. He would do all he

could to protect everything he loved so dearly: the ponies, this yard, his home and his beloved Flying Fillies.

They had an event that afternoon, and as always they would plaster on their smiles. If only those watching knew exactly what it was like when the music stopped.

Chapter 1

Thirteen year old Alice Smalley patted the neck of her red roan pony, Secret, as he stood quietly during a championship class. It had been another successful day for her mum's show team. Alice loved every one of the horses at Park Farm, the family's competition yard, but it was Secret who held a special place in her heart.

She smiled as Secret flicked an ear back, as

if listening to her thoughts. The bond between the two was unbreakable. Secret had been hard work – he was stubborn and headstrong – but Alice had worked tirelessly training him, and her effort was paying off. Now, at almost six years of age, the future was looking very bright for the talented gelding.

The judge smiled, calling the pair forward into first place. No one was surprised; Secret was a born show pony. He'd inherited the good looks of his dam, Lily, and the flamboyant personality of his sire, Carlamu Rowan. Secret didn't just trot, he *floated*. When he entered the ring his eyes sparkled and he lapped up the attention. The bigger the audience, the better he performed.

"Redgrove Secret," the commentator said over the loudspeaker, "trained and produced by Alice Smalley!"

Grinning, Alice nudged her pony into a

canter, Secret's long strides eating up the ground and his crimson mane flying. The crowd clapped and cheered, full of admiration for the real-life red Pegasus and his talented rider...

"*Alice!*" Josephine Smalley's shrill voice cut sharply through Alice's thoughts, and she jumped, feeling guilty. "All OK?" Josephine peered at her daughter, and then, without waiting for an answer, was back to business. "Come on," she said bossily, "there's still Lachlan's second class to go and you need to hurry. Go, and good luck!"

Alice sighed heavily. She had been completely lost in her daydream. But here she was at the side of the ring, clutching the reins of Porridge, her faithful Shetland. Secret was still out in his paddock at home. He was nowhere near ready for a championship class, and Alice knew it. There were days she couldn't even get him to walk *into* an arena, even in hand, let alone canter

around one as the winner, and so far every show they had attended to had been a disaster one way or another.

Automatically Alice's hand touched the curved pink scar on her cheek, as it did whenever she thought about how the little gelding had come to her. If it hadn't been for Secret, Alice would never have gone near a horse again. The scar would always remind her of her accident with Honey, the worst day of her life. A simple cross-country ride on a crisp Christmas Eve had ended in tragedy after Honey had fallen at a jump and died, and Alice had been badly injured. It had been no one's fault; Honey's big heart had simply given up. Over time the memory had grown easier to live with, but Alice owed Secret everything.

Alice gave Porridge a final pat before sprinting off to complete her last ridden class, trying not to roll her eyes. Show days were everything to her

7

mum, and she was always uptight.

Josephine Smalley, Alice's mum, was a highly respected showing producer, and Alice had played a big part in the yard's success, winning just about every championship out there. There was a long waiting list of people who were desperate to send her mum their best ponies to train and compete. As a result, Alice always had wonderful ponies to ride. A few riders on the circuit resented this, saying that Alice only had to sit there and collect rosettes, and that it didn't take any real skill. So Alice was desperate to prove herself both as a good rider *and* as a trainer, and Secret was her chance. The little roan was hers, and hers alone. But Alice had to admit she was struggling with the spirited red pony.

Moments later, mounted on Lachlan, a magnificent Highland, Alice's thoughts drifted to her mum. Alice often wished she could have a

regular pony club mum, and that they had time for other stuff, like fun rides and cross-country rallies. But ever since Alice's fall Josephine had been cautious about Alice doing anything risky. Alice often thought back to how alive and free she had felt galloping cross-country on her beloved mare, right before her world had come crashing down. She had very nearly given up riding for good, and it had only been the chance arrival of Secret that had encouraged her back to her true love, ponies.

A few years had passed since then, and Alice had qualified numerous ponies for the Horse of the Year Show and Olympia. Every spare surface in the Smalley's kitchen was covered with sashes and rosettes. Josephine lived and breathed showing, taking ponies all over the country to compete in flat ridden classes. Her speciality was mountain and moorland classes, where the ponies competed against others of the same breed.

It required a huge amount of work to school the ponies to this high standard, and most weekends were spent riding them at the shows.

But Alice was growing tired of the show ring. It wasn't that she didn't enjoy riding the ponies, but showing was never what Alice had been into. Before her fall she had been hoping to join the local pony club. But Alice's confidence had taken such a knock that it had seemed simpler to help her mum out and concentrate solely on the showing. Now that's all she did: the same thing week after week.

Alice dreamed about a weekend when there was nothing to do but gallop Secret along a beach. Secret was the reason she rode again, although she was trying to ignore the small voice inside her, which was questioning whether she would *ever* be able to ride him properly at all. She sighed, nudging Lachlan forward. It was all such a mess!

Chapter 2

Lachlan cantered easily ahead of his competitors. He was one of the best-known ponies in the country, and was heading towards a well-earned retirement in the next couple of years. The big Highland was very special to Alice. Lachlan was the first pony she had ridden after her accident with Honey, and he had taken good care of her.

Smiling, the judge called Alice into first place,

to a smattering of applause from the ringside. Pinning the red rosette to Lachlan's bridle, Alice thanked the judge and set off on a lap of honour. As they cantered around, Alice gave the gelding a deserved pat and wondered how many times they had done this. One hundred, two hundred? She'd lost count. She knew it made her sound spoilt, but winning in the show ring just wasn't exciting any more.

★

Alice yawned as she climbed the steps into the horsebox. She had helped Shelley, the yard's assistant groom, rug up the ponies who were now munching on their hay nets ready for the journey. Josephine was making herself a cup of tea in the horsebox. It had been a good day and Alice could tell her mum was happy.

Alice hovered in the doorway, her shirt untucked and her boots replaced with trainers. Her hair,

white blonde and almost as pale as her skin, was escaping from its tightly wrapped bun, and stray tendrils drifted round her face.

"Mum?"

"Yes, sweetheart?" Her mum was now sitting down with her video camera.

"I just wondered if I could go down to the main ring for a bit."

"Sure." Her mum didn't even look up from the screen, carefully studying Lachlan's individual show. "But we need to leave at four. Stay on the horsebox side of the ring please, and take your mobile."

Alice checked her watch. Twenty precious minutes to herself! Sprinting through the line of horseboxes, she weaved in and out of the crowds, heading for the main ring. Flopping down on the grass, panting with exertion, she tucked her long legs underneath her as a familiar drum roll crashed around the arena.

The crowd was buzzing with excitement as the first rider galloped in. A young blonde woman in a hooded cloak, riding side-saddle on a huge grey. Bright feathers adorned the horse's mane. She was followed by a younger girl with curly brown hair. She stood astride a pair of chunky Dales ponies, who cantered merrily round the ring. Next came a tall sandy-haired man, who drew the biggest cheer from the crowd, particularly the girls. His horse was a gorgeous chestnut thoroughbred. The horse didn't have a saddle or bridle on, just a simple rope round his strong neck. Alice watched as the rider expertly used his seat and legs to control the powerful chestnut. Her mum would say his talent was wasted, that he should be in the show ring with a seat like that. Alice giggled to herself; she could hear her mum's bossy voice as clear as anything. Josephine was a real stickler for tradition

and turnout!

Then Alice straightened up as the final rider entered the ring. He was a boy of around fourteen and he had such presence that a ripple went through the crowd. His pony was a Highland, like Lachlan, but snow white. *He wouldn't look out of place in the show ring*, Alice thought as the pony cantered past her, an elaborate feather plume decorating his bridle. The rider, all in black, stared straight ahead, his dark brown hair brushing his eyes as the pony performed perfect leg changes.

Alice had watched the Flying Fillies display many times at shows up and down the country, and she knew the boy was by far the best rider in the group. He sat perfectly still in the saddle, and the horses he rode performed beautifully. But he rarely smiled, and had a sinister presence. Alice wondered if he was really so moody, or if it was all part of the act.

The team were now performing a scene from a play, each rider in a different role. The blonde girl on the grey pony was the damsel in distress, the sandy-haired boy was a handsome prince, and the girl on the Dales ponies was a court joker. And, as always, the dark-haired boy was the villain. The crowd whooped with delight as the riders galloped across the arena performing daredevil tricks, throwing themselves out of the saddle and vaulting back on and crossing each other's paths with millimetres to spare. Alice was completely transfixed. It was unbelievably exciting, a world away from the neat and proper show ring. She was so absorbed that she didn't hear her mobile ringing. Then she jumped as her mum called her name, pushing through the crowd to reach her.

"There you are." Her mum sounded irritated. "What on earth are you watching?"

Alice stood up reluctantly. The dark-haired boy

was in the middle of a perfectly executed vault, and the crowd was going wild.

"What is *this*?" her mum continued, wrinkling her nose. "What a waste of a super pony."

Alice frowned as she thought about why she loved the display. It wasn't just the freedom of the moves and the fun of the performance, but also the obvious rapport between the riders and ponies.

Alice looked at her mum. "Don't you think it's amazing? How they ride their ponies like that, and how the ponies respond? It must take loads of work."

With perfect timing, the boy in black thundered past, practically upside down in the saddle. Surely her mum must be a tiny bit impressed?

"Oh come on, Al," her mum said. "What *we* do takes loads of work: getting the ponies moving correctly, looking their best, doing what ponies should be doing. I mean, this is a bit of fun—"

she paused, frowning. "But it's just tricks, circus stuff!"

Alice looked at her mum's face – her mouth curled in a slight grimace – and sighed. She would never understand.

Glancing behind her as she reluctantly headed back to the lorry, for a split second Alice thought the boy in black was smiling and looking right at her. But when she looked again he was galloping in the other direction. She shook her head. It must have been her imagination.

Chapter 3

Alice climbed into the horsebox cab and settled down next to Shelley, ready for the long journey back home. Shelley was already asleep with *Horse and Hound* over her face.

After double-checking the map, Josephine put the key into the ignition, looking more cheerful. "Another good day. Well done, darling." She sounded pleased. "Hopefully the same again tomorrow. It'll be another long day."

Alice stared out of the window as her mum continued to talk about the show, wondering what the girls from school would be up to that weekend. She bet they wouldn't be driving to the opposite ends of the country two days in a row to ride ponies in the ring. Then Alice's thoughts drifted to the boy in black. Had he really looked at her? Hugging her knees to her chest, she was asleep before the lorry had even reached the road.

★

Alice's dad was waiting for them back at the yard. Completely unhorsey, Andrew Smalley was very relaxed about his family's dedication to showing, even though it meant he barely saw his wife or daughter over the summer. When the lorry pulled into the yard he was tinkering around with a piece of machinery.

Alice adored her dad. He worked in London,

but changed straight into overalls when he was home. Alice still wasn't exactly sure what he did, something to do with finance, but he always said he would rather be mending tractors. *A bit like me,* she thought, *out showing when I'd rather be galloping over the downs!*

"Looks like another winning day!" Her dad gestured to the red rosettes, and gave Alice a kiss on her forehead as she jumped down from the cab.

Alice stretched her tired limbs. They still had a couple of hours' work to get the ponies settled for the night, and the lorry repacked for the morning. Fergus, the head groom, came over to help. He was in his early twenties and lived above the stables. Fergus was like a big brother to Alice and he was just about the only person Josephine really trusted with the ponies, even more so than Alice.

Taking hold of Lachlan's lead rope, Fergus followed Alice and Porridge to the stables.

21

"How did you do today?" he asked.

Alice smiled, slipping off the Shetland's head collar and giving him a pat as he bustled into his stable. "All firsts."

Fergus grinned. "Awesome!"

He gave Lachlan a hug. Out of all the ponies, the gentle Highland was his favourite. He'd been bred by Fergus's late dad, up in Scotland. Fergus's brother, Rory, lived nearby and continued to breed a few ponies, keeping their father's famous Highland breeding lines going.

"And did you get to watch the Flying Fillies?"

Fergus was the only one who knew about Alice's love for the daredevil riders, and occasionally came with her to watch.

Alice nodded, grinning. She always felt a bubble of excitement when she realised the Flying Fillies would be at the same shows as her. They seemed so glamorous and free-spirited, a world away from

her life.

"Introduce yourself one day – you must be their biggest fan!" Fergus continued as he rugged Lachlan up, while Alice tended to Porridge. A low wall divided the stables, meaning the two ponies, the best of friends, were able to keep each other company.

Alice grimaced. "No way. They'd think I was some kind of stalker!"

Fergus winked. "Well, you said it…" he teased as Alice threw a handful of hay at him, much to his amusement.

★

After the ponies were settled, Alice went to see Secret. He was out in the paddock, grazing with Tudor, a Dartmoor gelding. Secret ambled over to Alice, nudging her with his soft nose.

Alice smiled at the memory of Georgia Black handing over Secret's lead rope, both girls crying, and the moment Alice realised Secret really was hers for ever. She leaned against Secret's side as he carried on eating, breathing in his sweet pony scent. Alice loved him so much that she had presumed training him would be easy, the strengthening of a magical bond, like she had read about in her pony books. But Secret was anything but easy. Although he seemed to enjoy being ridden, his progress wasn't consistent and it sometimes felt like one step forward and two steps back!

Sighing, she started to plait a section of Secret's mane. For a brief moment she thought about the dark-haired boy on the Highland and wondered what his life was like. Really amazing, she bet. Full of freedom and adventure. It seemed unlikely their paths would ever properly cross.

Chapter 4

As spring gave way to early summer, Alice remained caught up in the whirlwind of her mum's busy schedule. Josephine was keen they focus on the young ponies owned by their clients, and was looking for a new show rider to help out. They needed someone who would ride at shows for them and build a relationship with the ponies at home. With her mum's high standards it was proving difficult to find the right person. In the meantime, Alice was doing all the show riding on her own.

In a few days' time Secret was going to his very first ridden show, a small country fair. Before Alice had started riding him he had been to quite a few in-hand shows, and had seemed to enjoy the hustle and bustle, his eyes bright and shiny. But even then, actually going *into* the ring had been a different story. Secret had refused to trot in every single one of his classes, and sometimes he wouldn't move altogether. It was as if he shut down as soon as he went into the ring. Alice still felt the burn of shame as she remembered a steward at one particular show, an elderly man in a bowler hat, limping behind the pair and waving his spotty handkerchief as he tried to encourage Secret forward. Secret had just yawned and closed his eyes and Alice had come last. She remembered

the judge's words – *the most gorgeous pony on the showground, but such a naughty boy!*

Alice was hoping that Secret would be better now that she was riding him, and after watching the pair trot a wobbly circle in the arena at home Josephine had entered them into a novice ridden class. Alice would be competing alongside family ponies and her mum was judging at another show, so Fergus was taking her instead. The pressure was off and Alice was hoping they would have fun.

★

A few days later, and the day before the show, Alice realised they might not even make it into the show ring!

"Please, Secret!"

Alice scratched the little pony on his withers as he blew hard out of his nostrils, every hair on his body quivering as he snorted at some unseen monster. Alice was practising her show in the school, a simple figure of eight and a canter circle on both reins. Secret was being particularly naughty, either refusing to move or spooking wildly at everyday objects, like the coat draped over the fence. Alice found herself growing increasingly anxious.

Alice was the only one who could catch Secret, and the only one who could load him on to the lorry. He would follow her anywhere. But the minute she tried any sort of training, he changed!

Nervously she gathered up the reins again, then nudging him softly forward, she asked him to walk on. If they could manage a nice circle in walk and trot, that would be enough for the day. Secret yawned, and rested a back leg. He wasn't going to move. Trying not to dig her heels in, Alice felt a familiar wave of frustration wash over her. She had waited more than four years to ride him, and thought they had built up a great relationship. He lived in the best yard in the country. He was in

brilliant health and his tack fitted perfectly. He had been easy to back and ride away. So *why* was it all going wrong now?

"Come *o-n*!" Alice said through gritted teeth. It was so tempting to pick up a crop and give him a wallop but she knew that would do more harm than good. Feeling like she might scream, Secret chose that moment to turn round to look at her, fluttering his eyelashes and nibbling her boot gently. Alice was overcome by love for him once again. However naughty he was, he could still melt her heart.

"Come on, boy," she said again, softer this time. Secret pricked his ears forward and decided to walk on. After a wobbly lap of the school Alice relaxed and patted him. It wasn't great, but it was a start: they had sort of achieved something.

Fergus had been watching from the side of the arena. "You know," he called to Alice, "we can just take him to the fair for the experience. You could ride him in the warm-up for a bit and see how he gets on. He doesn't have to go in the class."

Alice nodded. Fergus always made sensible suggestions. She tried to smile at the older groom. "OK, that sounds like a very good idea!"

★

Once Alice had put Secret back into his stable she settled down to clean his tack, running her hand over the nut-brown leather and breathing in its familiar comforting scent. It was Alice's favourite horsey job, calming her down and giving her time to think. She was so lost in her thoughts that she gave a start as Shelley bustled in, humming cheerfully to herself and hunting through the pile of saddlecloths.

"Hey, Al!" Shelley grinned. "Looking forward to tomorrow?"

Alice made a face. "Sort of," she mumbled. "If

Secret behaves."

She didn't want to say too much in case Shelley passed anything on to her mum.

"You'll be fine!" Shelley said breezily, finding the cloth she wanted.

"You think?" Alice replied, trying to sound casual.

"Yeah." Shelley was halfway out of the door and whistled for Poppy the dog to follow her. "You're overthinking it. Try to think of him as one of the yard ponies. He's just a pony at the end of the day."

Alice considered this. Yes, he was, but he was also her pony, her *special* pony, and she wanted everyone to see how well she had done with him. She wanted everything to be perfect!

Chapter 5

There was a shrill whinny from the back of the horsebox, and Alice felt the vehicle shake as Fergus pulled up at a set of traffic lights. As well as Secret, they were also taking Porridge the Shetland to the show, and a sweet Fell pony called Archie. Josephine was training Archie for a new client, a woman who was married to a former footballer. Alice had never heard of the footballer, but Fergus

had told her he was once super famous. Alice was more interested in the client's pony. Archie was gorgeous and showed huge potential. He had such wonderful manners compared to Secret, she thought disloyally. Secret had spent all morning trying to chew Archie's mane!

As they parked, everyone turned to stare at their huge black lorry that looked out of place among the trailers towed by family estates. Alice scanned the showground. There were a few ponies being trotted about, but it all felt very low-key.

★

After unloading the ponies from the box, Alice rode a lap of the showground without any major incidents. Secret felt responsive, his ears pricked forward, and Alice's confidence increased. Giving him a pat, she made a thumbs-up sign at Fergus, who was combing out Archie's tail.

"OK?" he grinned.

Alice nodded. "Think so..." she replied. She tried to smile.

"Why don't you try your class?" Fergus continued. "There's only three in it. And you don't even have to canter, if you don't want to."

"OK," Alice responded, taking a deep breath. Gathering up Secret's reins she followed Fergus down to the pony rings, and took her place behind the two other competitors. They looked horrified as Alice entered the ring, and feeling a little embarrassed she tried to smile at them. She knew Secret was a beautiful pony, and that she was an experienced rider, but the class *was* for novice ponies ... and Secret was *definitely* a novice!

But as they circled the ring Alice frowned. Secret felt different. He had his ears back, something he very rarely did, and he seemed lacklustre, eyeing the exit every time they passed it. But he was called in first and Alice had a minute to settle him while

the judges chatted among themselves.

Peeling off a glove with her teeth, and leaning forward so she could adjust Secret's bridle, Alice was suddenly aware of the little roan's ears pricking up.

Fergus spotted it first, a bright blue balloon drifting slowly across the warm-up area and into the ring. There were some snorts and eye-rolls from the waiting horses, but nothing more. The two ponies next to her watched with mild interest.

Not Secret.

"Alice, turn him!"

But Fergus's warning came a fraction too late. As the balloon drifted upwards on a sudden gust, it came within centimetres of the line-up. The reins were ripped clean out of Alice's hands as Secret shot forward before wheeling round, sending Alice flying to the ground. Secret galloped straight out of the ring – ignoring the steward's frantic arm waving – and through the warm-up area, scattering alarmed ponies. Frozen, Alice could only watch from the ground as her pony disappeared. A judge ran over to check she was OK.

From the side of the ring Fergus sprang into action, jolting Alice to her senses as she scrambled up, her left hand burning where the reins had ripped through it. The other riders in her class looked on in astonishment. Secret might have been gorgeous, but at least their ponies were behaving!

Shouting an apology to the shocked judge, Alice ran after Fergus, realising that Secret had no intention of stopping at the barrier between the lorry park and the main show area. Shortening his stride, ears pricked, he neatly jumped the rope and carried on. Alice could tell that he was enjoying his adventure. He paused briefly to eat the flowers next to the tea tent where the officials were enjoying lunch. A woman ran out, waving her hat in anger

as Secret joyfully kicked up his heels and carried on. A group of men tried to form a circle round him, but Secret was too quick for them.

"This is a disaster!" Fergus swore grimly as he and Alice carried on in pursuit. They were gaining on Secret, but he had turned the chase into a game.

Alice felt tears trickle down her face, a mixture of shock, humiliation and frustration at not being able to catch her pony. She loved Secret more than anything, but at the moment she wasn't sure if she liked him one little bit! To her horror Secret was now trotting towards the entrance to the main ring, where a pony club jump-off was taking place. A loose pony among the showjumpers would spell disaster.

Then, like a miracle, a dark-haired boy stepped out from behind one of the marquees. Giving a long, low whistle, he held his hand out to Secret, who stopped dead, turning his head towards the boy. The little roan snorted, his eyes wary. The boy took one step forward, and Alice fully expected Secret to toss his head and carry on, but instead something amazing happened. Secret took a step towards the boy. The boy smiled, and took another step. Again, Secret did the same, lowering his head. His eyes were bright, totally fixed on the boy. Gradually and quietly, as Secret mirrored each step, the boy got closer until he held Secret's trailing reins. There was some relieved laughter from the watching crowd.

Secret's sides were heaving with exertion, but his ears were pricked and his eyes were sparkling. Giving a deep sigh, he rubbed his head against the boy, who chuckled. Shielding her own eyes against the sunshine, Alice gave a gasp of recognition. Secret's mystery catcher was the dark-haired rider from the Flying Fillies!

Chapter 6

The boy continued to fuss over Secret, who stood quietly next to him, resting his chin on the boy's shoulder in adoration. Alice felt herself go hot and cold as she realised how disastrous Secret's escape could have been. He could have knocked over a child, or caused an accident, or escaped on to the road.

Wiping away tears and sweat with the back

of her grubby hands, Alice could only stammer a thank-you. There were several angry-looking stewards approaching, and Fergus went over to talk to them, leaving Alice and Secret alone with the boy.

"That's one way to make an impression," he said, raising an eyebrow as he gathered up Secret's reins and handed them to Alice.

Alice couldn't think of anything to say. She could only stare down at his hands. They were outdoor hands, she found herself thinking irrationally, showing years of riding and mending fences and mucking out. Her own hand was stinging, and she carefully picked up Secret's reins, trying to look more confident than she felt.

Fergus jogged back, looking stressed. "I've sorted it, Alice. I apologised. I said Secret was spooked by a balloon. I think they'll let us off." He squinted back to the line of trailers. "I must go and

check Archie and Porridge," he continued. "Come on, let's get Secret back."

Wincing, Alice tried to turn Secret round. He leaned against her, rubbing his head up and down in delight. After his adventure it seemed he had no intention of moving anywhere. Noticing her hand, the boy took back the reins. Alice didn't stop him.

"I'll help her," he said to Fergus, who had already started to jog back to the abandoned ponies.

"Thanks," Fergus called over his shoulder.

"I'm Finn," the boy said, turning to look at Alice.

Alice muttered her own name in response, realising just how dark Finn's eyes were, and how they were framed by the thickest, longest eyelashes she had ever seen. She felt her cheeks burn, mortified at how she must look. Hair all over the place, face tomato-red and sweaty. But the worst thing was how treacherously Secret was behaving; Finn just clucked at him, and the little roan followed as meekly as a lamb.

"How did you manage that?" Finn sounded amused as he walked by the gelding's side, placing a hand casually on his neck. "You should really train your pony to come back to you, you know. You could use a whistle, like a sheepdog."

"Yes, thanks for that. Very helpful," Alice snapped.

She knew Finn was only teasing her, but she felt herself growing defensive, all her embarrassment and humiliation turning to anger. Unable to think of a further response, she glared at him instead, at the same time envying the casual way he led her pony. Secret walked quietly next to Finn, not even trying to snatch mouthfuls of grass or gaze at ponies they passed. To make matters worse, even when they passed a girl holding an enormous bunch of balloons Secret barely glanced at them. *Typical*.

A PONY called SECRET

Finn gave a whistle as he spotted Josephine's horsebox. "Alice in her palace," he grinned. "Nice lorry."

Alice wished they had used the trailer instead.

Fergus already had Archie tacked up. Groaning, Alice realised she still had to ride Archie in his class. She mounted carefully, taking up the reins, before visibly wincing as the Fell thrust his nose forward. Fergus frowned.

"It's my hand," Alice explained miserably, turning her palm over to show Fergus, who grimaced as he examined the angry red burn. "The reins ripped through it when I fell."

Archie was sweet, but if the young pony spooked, she just didn't have the strength to hold him.

"Well, you can't ride with an injured hand," Finn said thoughtfully. "Why don't you let me?"

Startled, Fergus turned to him. "Really? Have

you ever done a ridden show?"

"No," Finn said breezily as he moved closer to Archie, patting the handsome pony. "But how hard can it be?" He turned to Alice with a small smile. "And anyway, *you've* watched me ride often enough."

Alice was mortified. So he *had* noticed her watching his display events!

She took a deep breath and turned to Fergus. "He's one of the Flying Fillies. He is good. Really good." Flustered, she realised Finn was watching her closely.

A look of recognition dawned on Fergus's face. "Yes, of course," he said slowly. "Alice watches your show at pretty much every event we go to."

"Fergus!" Alice groaned. Honestly, he was worse than a big brother at times.

Finn grinned. "I know," he said, looking pleased

with himself. "So, what do you think?" he asked Fergus.

Alice looked expectantly at Fergus, willing him to say yes. They *could* go home without taking Archie into his class, but his owner would be very disappointed. Alice knew her mum trusted Fergus enough to make decisions on her behalf. Sometimes they had to draft in extra riders on show days, so what was the difference here?

Fergus hesitated. "Archie does need riding. I'll tell you what, ride him around the warm-up, and if he's OK, you can take him in the ring. It's a bit different to … um … what you normally do."

"We'll be fine," Finn said with a touch of arrogance. "My jods and boots will do, got any spare show kit?"

"There's a jacket, tie and hat in the lorry," Alice piped up.

She wasn't quite sure what to make of Finn, but

she had to admit she was excited to see how Archie would go with him. She had never seen Secret react to anyone like he had with Finn. She wanted to know what made him so special.

★

Finn quickly pulled on the jacket that had been hanging in the lorry wardrobe.

"Bit different from my normal get-up," he said with a frown. "Doesn't it get uncomfortable, wearing all this stuff?"

"A bit, I guess." Alice couldn't think of anything better to say. Finn seemed to have some weird effect on her, making her brain all sludgy.

Finn swung lightly into Archie's saddle and seemed to soothe the novice pony straight away, as he trotted quietly around the collecting ring. Fergus visibly relaxed as Finn sat still in the saddle, his hands light. Watching, Alice started to feel a twinge of envy that grew and grew. She thought

she was a good rider. But she began to wonder if it really *was* because she had always had such well-trained ponies. Secret was a whole new challenge. She loved him more than anything, but what if she just wasn't good enough to train him?

★

If Alice and Fergus had been impressed with Finn's riding in the warm-up, his performance in the show ring was even better. The class was quiet, but there was tension between a few of the ponies. Finn talked quietly to Archie under his breath, circling him away from the others, keeping him calm.

"What a lovely rider." Fergus, eyes narrowed, was watching the pair intently. "I wonder..."

"What?" Alice glanced at the groom, who was looking thoughtful.

"Oh, nothing. Just thinking out loud."

Archie trotted and cantered obediently to Finn's

light aids, ears pricked forward, a perfect picture of harmony between horse and rider.

Alice rubbed Secret's face as they watched, and he lowered his head happily. "That will be you and me soon, sweetheart," she whispered. "At least, I hope it will."

Then she frowned, realising she couldn't be so sure about that any more.

Chapter 7

No one was surprised when Finn and Archie were placed first. Archie looked so proud of himself that everyone around Fergus and Alice chuckled. Alice heard Fergus breathe a sigh of relief next to her.

Jumping off Archie with a grin, Finn handed the reins back to Fergus, along with the borrowed clothes. "I told you it would be OK," he said, giving Archie a hug. Then with an amused smile he turned to Alice and Secret. "You might want to keep hold of your pony next time. I can't guarantee I'll always be on hand to catch him!"

Alice glared at Finn. "It was a one-off incident," she said hotly. "What are you anyway, some kind of horse whisperer?"

Finn laughed. "Something like that!" Striding off, he gave a cheerful wave. "Oh, Alice in her palace, you might want to check the back of your jods."

Crossly Alice turned round to look at the back of her cream trousers. They were streaked with brown. She must have landed in a pile of muck in the ring when Secret bolted. No wonder the landing had been soft. Groaning with embarrassment, Alice buried her face in Secret's neck. When she looked up, Finn had gone.

★

For the next couple of weeks Alice tried to forget

about Finn and deliberately avoided his event at the next show they went to.

Alice had also begged Fergus not to tell her mum about Secret's escapades and Fergus had agreed, on the understanding that Alice did some more work with her pony before his next show. And so Alice continued her attempts at schooling, but quietly fantasised about galloping bareback up a meadow, hopping over fallen logs.

★

It was a rarity: a Sunday without a show in the diary. Alice's mum and dad were at a judge's lunch. It was Fergus's day off and the show ponies were all getting turned out into the fields for a rest day. Alice was planning on taking Secret for a ride in the top meadow, perhaps even jumping a few of the small logs up there. Then she could laze around for the rest of the afternoon, hanging out with her pony.

Unfortunately her mum had other ideas.

"I'm not leaving you here on your own," she said firmly.

"Oh, Mum, I'll be *fine*. Please?" Alice pleaded.

"No," her mum said in a tone that suggested Alice shouldn't try to answer back. "I've asked Fergus if you can go with him while he delivers a pony for his brother."

Alice scuffed the floor with her boots, scowling. Great. Her one day off from showing and she would be stuck in the horsebox all afternoon instead.

★

"All right?" Fergus said to Alice as he pulled away from Park Farm. She nodded, pulling a piece of hay from her hair, having just made up the evening hay nets.

They soon arrived at Fergus's brother's yard and quickly had the pony, a beautiful mouse dun mare, loaded into the van. To Alice's relief, the onward

journey to the pony's new home was short. She might even get back to work on Secret, if Fergus didn't take too long.

As they approached Rookham Manor, the pony's new home, Alice gaped. At the end of the drive was a seriously impressive old manor house, although it was a bit run-down. The ponies were stabled in an old coaching block nearby. The air was still, only broken up by the distant hum of bees in the meadows surrounding the yard.

"Hmmm. I expected someone to be here to meet us. Al, would you mind seeing if you can find someone, and I'll check on the mare?"

"Sure." Alice hopped down from the cab, pleased she had put shorts on that morning. It was a scorching hot day and the manor house shimmered and swam in the air like a mirage.

"Hello?"

Alice's voice echoed around the empty yard as

several ponies watched with mild interest from the cool of their stables. It suddenly dawned on Alice that she recognised the ponies. The Highland, the big grey, two matching Dales... It couldn't be, could it? Holding her breath, she peered into the gloom of a barn.

"We don't owe you anything!"

Startled, Alice moved forward, squinting into the darkness.

"My name's Alice, Alice Smalley," she called out, looking nervously around. This was seriously weird. "I'm here with Fergus. We have a pony for you?"

Emerging from a corner, a dark-haired boy glowered at her. It was Finn. Alice felt a blush rise to her pale cheeks.

"Hi ... Finn," she said, trying to sound cool. "We have your new pony—"

She felt the words die on her lips as Finn glared

at her with such fury that she started to back out of the barn. Luckily Fergus now stood behind her. He had an older girl with him, the blonde who rode the big grey. Alice felt as if she were meeting a famous pop star!

"Finn, this is the new pony I told you about. Marcus said we need—" the girl started, but Finn cut across her.

"Marcus always says," he snapped, stalking out of the barn without a backwards glance as the girl stared after him.

She sighed. "Don't mind him. Finn's always mad about something. Teenagers, eh?"

Reaching out to Alice, the girl shook her hand, smiling. She was in her early twenties and very pretty. "I'm Sasha," she said. She was wearing a black skirt and cowboy boots, and her blonde hair was tangled and woven with flowers. "Shall we get my new girl settled in?"

Alice scuffed her feet in the yard as Sasha and Fergus unloaded the Highland and sorted out the paperwork. Finn was nowhere to be seen. It was bad enough crashing into him at the country fair, but meeting like this, when there was clearly something going on between him and Sasha, felt really awkward.

Alice's heart sank as Fergus came to find her a few minutes later, looking stressed. "Sorry, Al, just my luck," he said in exasperation. "Lorry won't start; I've called the rescue truck but we could be stuck here for a bit."

Alice groaned. Her dreams of an afternoon with Secret were slipping away. But if Finn had disappeared, she could use the opportunity to get up close to the ponies. They were her horsey heroes after all!

"Oh no, what a shame!" Sasha appeared by Fergus's side, sounding anything but sorry as she

smiled up at the head groom. "Fergus, can you come and help me measure the new pony? I want to see what costumes we need to make up, or if we have anything that will fit."

"Sure!"

Fergus seemed keen to help, and Alice giggled to herself. At least someone was having fun!

Left alone again, Alice wandered around the pretty yard and said hello to the ponies, sort of hoping she might bump into Finn again. She patted the sweet pair of Dales ponies, the chestnut thoroughbred and the gorgeous dapple grey Sasha usually rode. He looked like an Irish Draught and was huge, over seventeen hands. The stables themselves were in need of repair and the whole yard had an air of faded glamour, like an old movie star. But Alice had to admit the yard blew her away. It was so different, so romantic, not a solarium or manège in sight, just beautiful historic buildings and flower meadows and gorgeous ponies. She loved it.

"Hello, sweetheart." Alice paused next to the snow-white Highland that Finn rode. The pony snuffled against her hands, his velvet muzzle a contrast to his bristly whiskers, and she laughed as he searched her pockets for treats.

"How are you, my darling?" she said chattily to the friendly pony, tracing the letters on his nameplate on the stable door. "Horatio," she smiled. "A fine name for a lovely pony."

Then she jumped as Finn emerged from the other side of the stable where he had been sorting out rugs. He had an unsettling way of looking straight at her, unblinking, so that her gaze fell first.

"Do you always talk to yourself?" he said, but there was the faintest hint of a smile on his lips.

Alice tried to think of a witty response, but couldn't. "You like Highlands then?" she said

finally, kicking herself inside. What a lame thing to say!

Finn raised an eyebrow at her. "I like all ponies."

When Alice asked Finn what his plans were for the new Highland mare a look of fury clouded his face.

"Well, we'll have to find enough money to look after her, for a start," Finn hissed, his eyes flashing. "But that doesn't worry *Marcus*."

Alice must have looked confused, and Finn sighed. "Sasha's my sister," he explained, "and Marcus is her boyfriend. He's the one that rides the chestnut. He joined last year. He's nothing but—"

He was interrupted by the arrival of Sasha and Fergus. Now Alice could see that Finn and Sasha did look alike, with the same high slanted cheekbones and long eyelashes, although Sasha's hair was as light as Finn's was dark. Finn's mood seemed to worsen when he saw his sister. Ignoring

Fergus and Alice he started arguing with her.

"Why did you buy the mare?" he hissed. "You know we can't afford her."

Looking uncomfortable, Sasha tried to diffuse the situation. "That's not true, Finn," she hissed back, her cheeks colouring. "Really, it's not," she said, turning to Fergus. "She's all paid for."

Fergus held up his hands, and shrugged. "I'm sure," he said. "Rory wouldn't sell a pony without a cleared cheque."

Stomping off, Finn muttered under his breath. Although Alice couldn't be sure, she thought she heard the words "gullible" and "naive" and something about paying winter feed bills. Sasha ignored her younger brother and soon she and Fergus were deep in conversation again, and Finn was gone.

Chapter 8

Alice wasn't sure why, but something made her slip off quietly and go and find Finn. He was sitting in the paddock, throwing a tennis ball for a lurcher.

Alice sat down beside him as he continued throwing the ball, not looking at her. They sat in silence for a few minutes, the sun warm on Alice's face, before Finn spoke.

"She's a lovely mare," he said, his voice flat. "I

expect you think she should be in a show ring, don't you, doing boring circles?"

"No." Alice patted the dog as he dropped the ball. That might be what her mum would think, but not her. "Why did your sister buy the pony?" she asked.

"Because Marcus told her to," Finn growled. "Everything's gone wrong since he joined the Flying Fillies. At first I thought he was OK. I mean, he can ride well enough. But—" he looked round as he said this, as if to check no one was listening "—I don't think he's got any interest in the team. Apart from what he can get out of it."

"What do you mean?"

Finn looked grim. "I heard him on the phone; he said the team was a waste of time and that Sasha was loaded, which she's absolutely *not*." He glanced at Alice. "He's up to something. But Sash doesn't believe me. He came along and swept her

A PONY called SECRET

off her feet and now she thinks he's the answer to all our problems."

He looked around him, at the crumbling stable yard and the wildflower meadows. "He's *crazy* if he thinks he can get his hands on any of this," he said, his jaw tense.

"Do you both live here then?" Alice asked. Sasha was obviously older than Finn but she still seemed very young to have the responsibility of such a big house and yard. Finn nodded.

"Just you two?" Alice couldn't help herself. "What about your parents?" she blurted out.

Pain flashed across Finn's face. "Well, Mum's dead," he said shortly, and Alice's hands flew to her mouth.

"Oh, Finn, I'm really sorry, I didn't mean—"

Before she could continue, Finn put his hand up, his expression softening. "It's OK, how were you meant to know? You don't know me." He looked

★
★
63
★

straight at her as he said this.

"What about your dad then?" Alice asked carefully.

"Dad's a horse trainer," Finn explained. "He's into natural horsemanship and stuff like that. Not your thing I expect," he added dismissively.

Alice frowned. "How do you know? *You* don't know *me*."

Finn gave a small smile. "Touché. Well, Dad's speciality is difficult horses. The sort that won't respond to anyone else; he just seems to be able to communicate with them somehow. Horatio was totally unrideable when we got him. He bucked his owner off every day and he was going to be put down: they thought he was dangerous. Dad turned him round, gained his trust. All Horatio wanted was someone to listen to him."

Alice was fascinated. She couldn't help but wonder what Finn's dad would make of Secret.

"We did all the normal pony stuff growing up. Mum would take us to pony club and shows, that sort of thing," Finn continued. "But when Dad went away to teach in Spain, he came across some stunt riders and told us all about it. That was that: we were hooked. We never really fitted in at pony club anyway," he added with a small chuckle.

Alice listened as Finn explained how his parents had set up the display team, using their brilliant horsemanship skills to train the ponies.

"It started off with just a bridle, then a rope round the neck." Finn's eyes sparkled as he spoke, and once again Alice was struck by just how handsome he was. "Getting the ponies to really trust us. It's hard to explain. Dad just seems to ask horses to do things, and they respond." He smiled and paused, a faraway look on his face, and Alice wondered what he was thinking about.

"You and Sasha are both amazing riders,"

Alice said, thinking back to all the times she had watched them.

"There's nothing like the feeling of standing up on your pony's back for the first time." Finn said, his smile growing. "And then we got more daring, and taught ourselves other tricks. The Flying Fillies was just taking off when Mum died…" His voice faltered. "That's why it means so much to keep it going."

"Where's your dad now?" Alice knew she was asking lots of personal questions, but she couldn't help herself.

Finn looked away. "After the funeral Dad took off," he said eventually, keeping his voice steady. "He couldn't make Mum better. But he *can* make horses better."

Alice felt tears prick the corners of her eyes.

Finn explained that his dad had found various jobs along the way, at Montana ranches, Argentine

polo farms and Kenyan horse safaris, sending back money each month.

"What, enough money to keep this huge house and the yard going?" Alice asked in surprise.

"Luckily there's no mortgage or we'd never manage," Finn said. "The house will belong to us when we're older, but the stable yard already belongs to Sasha. When our grandmother died a couple of years ago, we moved down from the north and took over the place. But even with Dad's money and the display money we're only just making enough to feed and care for the horses." Finn gave a resigned sigh. "Sash has big plans for the Flying Fillies, but we need to replace the costumes and all the tack is ancient and falling apart."

Alice had never heard anything like Finn's story in her life. She couldn't believe their dad had taken off like that, to ride horses all over the world. And now Finn and Sasha travelled up and down the country for their displays, living alone in this glorious house. It was a whole new world!

"Is your dad ever coming back?" she asked, totally absorbed in Finn's story.

"I don't know when he'll be back," Finn said, plucking at the grass. "He just needed to get away. Mum's death hit him hard. It was hard for all of us. But we manage, Sasha and me."

"But … you're both so young," Alice said. She couldn't help it.

Finn snorted, narrowing his eyes. "I'm fourteen, hardly young. You don't need to feel sorry for me."

"Alice!" A whistle made her jump. It was Fergus, waving from the yard. "Lorry's fixed!" he bellowed, indicating for her to come and join him.

Reluctantly Alice stood up. "Good luck with your new pony," she said. She wasn't sure what else she could say.

"Thanks. See you around. And good luck with Secret."

Finn had already stood up, heading back to the stables. Alice watched him go, his dark head held high, his lurcher by his side.

★

As Alice and Fergus trundled back down the long drive a few minutes later, Alice squinted through the late-afternoon sun and spotted a pony and rider in one of the meadows. Finn and Horatio. The pony had no saddle or bridle, yet was cantering the most perfect circle, Finn's hands entwined in his mane. Alice could only stare.

Fergus slowed the lorry right down, hands over his eyes to shield them from the sun as he watched. He gave a long whistle. "That boy sure can ride," he said. "Alice, I've had an idea…"

Chapter 9

A few days later Alice had just arrived back from school when her mum called her over. She was in the yard, wearing jeans and a faded pink shirt. Alice much preferred her mum when she was like this, relaxing with the ponies and Poppy the dog.

"What, Mum?" she asked curiously. Josephine looked unusually pleased.

"I think Fergus has found us our new show

rider!" her mum said in a satisfied voice, and Alice felt her stomach flip. She suddenly knew exactly what her mum was about to say.

"The boy, the one who rode Archie when your classes clashed at the fair."

Alice was startled. She'd forgotten to ask Fergus how he'd explained Finn riding Archie!

"Fergus said he was exceptional," Josephine continued. "And then I hear he was the one you delivered the pony for. I asked around, and he rides for something called the Flying Fillies. Is that the silly thing you were watching a few weeks ago?" She had a look of bemusement as she said this. "Anyway, I thought I'd offer him, Finn Cutler, the riding job. I haven't found anyone else, and it sounds like he might do very well in a *proper* riding discipline!"

Alice winced. Her mum could be pretty blunt at times.

"Fergus gave me their number, and Finn has agreed to a trial ride," Josephine said, glancing at her watch. "He should be here any minute now."

"What?" Alice's hands flew to her mouth in horror. There was no time to change out of her detested school uniform: a maroon knee-length kilt and blazer. Then she kicked herself for caring so much, but she hadn't been able to stop thinking about Finn.

Just then there was a beep as the electric gates opened and a battered Land Rover pulled into the yard. Sasha was in the driver's seat, some sort of elaborate headdress on her mass of blonde hair, and Finn was in the passenger side. As he got out, Alice saw he was also in his school uniform, a navy polo shirt, but he had a way of making it look cool. He gave her a little smile.

Josephine's mouth fell open as Sasha emerged. Not only was she wearing a sequinned hairband

decorated with large feathers, but her face was sprinkled with glitter.

"Hi!" Sasha said nonchalantly, her cowboy boots clicking on the cobbles as she reached forward to shake Josephine's hand with a big smile. "Oh! Don't mind me; I've just been working on some costumes, and didn't have time to change."

"Right," Alice's mum said faintly. She looked down in barely concealed horror at the glitter raining down from Sasha on to the sleeve of her pink shirt. Then briskly, she turned to Finn. "Hello," she said. "Fergus recommended you. I must say, I was a bit dubious. What you do is very … frivolous."

Alice winced again.

"Well, yes. We don't just trot round in circles," Sasha said defensively. "And my brother really can ride."

"Of course," Alice's mum said stiffly. "I suppose

the best thing we can do is see you up in the saddle."

She was uncharacteristically silent a short while later, as she watched Finn ride Archie in the arena. They completed the most elegant figure of eight on the lightest rein. Finn had the black pony dancing, and Alice was totally mesmerised.

"Very nice," Josephine said with a nod, taking hold of Archie's reins as Finn completed his ride. Any praise was rare, so Alice knew her mum was impressed! "When can you start?"

Finn shrugged. "Whenever," he replied.

Her mum nodded and turned to Sasha. "Well then, what about a couple of hours after school a few evenings a week and then shows at the weekend? We can work out lifts, and things like that."

Sasha nodded and smiled. "Sure," she said. "Finn knows the Flying Fillies routines inside out

so we don't need too much practice, though he has to help look after our horses, of course. I'll let you know the dates when we have shows, although there's not that many coming up..." Her voice trailed off and she looked worried for a moment. She turned to her brother. "Anyway, I think it would be good for you to have a focus. What do you say?"

Finn shrugged again. "Yeah, sounds OK."

Josephine flicked through her diary. "Well, I'll call you in the next day or so. Each week will depend on our schedule, and I'll pay you by the hour. Is that OK?"

Finn nodded, and they exchanged the briefest of handshakes.

Alice felt a huge range of emotions wash over her. She was now going to see Finn regularly. She still found him hard to read – but there was something intriguing about him. She thought about the boys from the neighbouring school that all the girls in her class fancied; to Alice they all looked and sounded the same. Finn was different.

As he climbed back into the Land Rover, Finn grinned at her, the first proper smile he'd ever given her. Her heart leapt, just a little bit. Perhaps he was going to say something nice…

"See you soon, Alice in her palace!" Finn laughed as Sasha pulled away in a cloud of dust.

★

As the season rolled on, the Smalley team continued their success, with all the ponies who had been aimed at the Horse of the Year Show gaining their tickets in good time. Finn had already delighted Josephine by qualifying a lovely New Forest pony called Coco in his first week. That meant they could let the experienced ponies have a bit of a break for the summer holidays, and concentrate on the younger ones. Alice and Finn would be

riding them at the smaller shows to build up their confidence.

Alice had more time to dedicate to Secret, and she was determined to make things better between them. One evening, she decided to school in the bottom meadow. At first it was OK. Secret trotted obediently in a circle, and Alice started to relax. But then he stopped, and refused to go forward. Backing up, Secret stared longingly in the direction of the fields that were going to be cut for hay. For one crazy second Alice thought about letting him gallop through the fields. It was as if Secret had read her mind and he eagerly surged forward, and Alice stopped him just in time. Her mum would kill her if he trampled all over the uncut grass. Finally Alice gave up and dismounted, slipping the reins over Secret's head and leading him back to his stable. She knew she shouldn't end their session on a negative note, but she had no idea what to do.

Secret was now almost six, and growing bigger and stronger. Alice didn't want to admit it, but she was becoming nervous around him. The balloon disaster had made her worry that she wasn't as good a rider as she thought. And now she had seen Finn in action, it was more obvious than ever that she still had a lot to learn!

Chapter 10

With Finn busy juggling schoolwork and pony care, Josephine sometimes took her ponies over to Rookham Manor for schooling sessions. On these days Josephine or Fergus would first collect Alice from school, and then Finn. Alice often wondered what he was like at school, he certainly had a 'don't mess with me' vibe. In fact, Alice wondered about Finn a lot, especially when she was meant to be doing other things, like homework or her chores.

Alice and Finn sat in awkward silence in the lorry during their journeys together, Finn staring out of the window and Alice desperate to make conversation but not sure what to say, especially with her mum listening in. Alice longed to be left alone at Finn's yard but her mum or Fergus always oversaw the schooling sessions, to check the ponies were going correctly.

Today Finn was schooling Archie. He was due to ride him at the next show, when Archie's owner would come to watch. Although she hadn't said it in so many words, Alice could tell her mum wanted to put her best rider on Archie to impress his owner. Even though Alice *knew* Finn was a better rider than her, it still hurt. She longed to have the same connection with Secret that Finn had with his ponies. He made it look so effortless.

She was so engrossed in watching that she didn't

realise someone had joined them at the side of the makeshift arena. It was Marcus, Sasha's boyfriend. Alice noticed Finn scowl at him as he rode by.

"You must be Mrs Smalley." Marcus offered his hand to Alice's mum, who shook it as Marcus flashed her a grin. It was easy to see why the crowds adored him on display days: he was really handsome. But Alice felt herself bristle; she just got the feeling he wasn't genuine.

"How *wonderful* for you to give Finn a chance." Marcus sighed. "After all, there's no future for him here."

Alice's mum looked a little confused. "But Finn and Sasha have lots going on with their stunt riding," she said, still watching Finn.

"Well, between you and me," Marcus continued in a stage whisper, "it's not amounting to very much. Sasha has been filling the boy's head with this dream of the Flying Fillies, but it's more like

81

the Flopping Fillies at the moment." He gave a little chuckle as if pleased with his own joke.

"That's not true!" Alice waded in, unable to stop herself. "I've been to loads of your displays. Everyone loves watching them!"

Marcus gave her an irritated look, as if he had just noticed her.

"*They* might," he said nastily, "but the show organisers don't. Too old-fashioned I expect. They want to book racing quad bikes or something more exciting. Believe me, I'm the one that does the bookings. It's been *impossible* this year to secure anything."

Alice glared at him, remembering what Finn had said about overhearing him on the phone, and Marcus calling the Flying Fillies a waste of time.

Marcus turned back to Josephine, ignoring Alice once again. "Well, anyway, I just think it's *so* great you're giving Finn this chance. He's been a bit of

a handful since his dad left, getting into trouble at school, that sort of thing. He was almost *expelled*," he added, raising his eyebrows theatrically. "Now it's the holidays, I'm sure if you have any extra hours available, both he and Sasha will be pleased with the extra money."

Josephine didn't look as if she liked Marcus, Alice was pleased to see. "Oh, right. Well, I'll bear that in mind."

"Thank you, Mrs Smalley," Marcus said, giving her the full benefit of his wide smile as he sauntered away. "I know Sasha will be very pleased."

Finn had finished warming down Archie and as he walked him back to the paddock fence, Alice noticed him shoot Marcus a murderous look.

"Go and get a drink of water, Finn," her mum said, taking hold of Archie's reins. "You look very hot."

With her mum looking after Archie, Alice slipped

off after Finn, who was filling up a mug from the yard hose. As usual Finn's presence made Alice feel clumsy and self-conscious.

"That all right?" he asked shortly. "Is your mum happy? Do I match her high standards?"

"Mum's really pleased," Alice said truthfully.

"Good. Archie's an awesome pony."

There was an awkward silence.

"So Marcus just said something weird." Alice lowered her voice, and Finn looked up sharply. "He told us that the shows aren't booking you any more."

"What?" Finn looked angry. "Every single event we've done has had amazing feedback. Sasha was having to turn down events last year because we were so busy!"

Alice frowned, thinking hard. "What's going on then?"

"Sasha *thinks* Marcus is working really hard to

get the events sorted," Finn growled.

"But you don't think he is?"

Finn looked at her for a few moments, his black eyes unreadable.

"Alice," he said finally. "When you leave here you go back to your perfect yard and perfect life and perfect school. Why are you even interested in what's going on with me?"

Alice blushed. "I was just trying to help!"

Finn looked straight at her. "You're right," he said finally. "Sorry, that was really rude of me. I'm just not used to anyone ... caring."

"Can't you..." Alice thought carefully about what she was about to say. "Can't you call your dad? If he knew there was stuff going on with the Flying Fillies, wouldn't he come home to help?"

"*That* is not an option," Finn said flatly. "Sasha won't let me call him; she says he's got enough on his plate. She thinks Marcus is going to sort everything, all our bills and debts and stuff. And although I can't prove anything yet – I have a feeling he wants to do the complete opposite. As far as I'm concerned, Marcus is a total loser, he—"

"Finn, that's enough!" Shaking with rage, Sasha appeared from behind the two teenagers, making Alice jump. "You've had it in for Marcus from the beginning!" Sasha snarled at her younger brother. "Marcus has been working really, really hard trying to get us bookings, so I can concentrate on the training! Finn, you need to get over yourself. You just hate the fact that now *he's* the one everyone comes to see!"

"That's not true," Finn shot back, his cheeks reddening. "I bet he told you that, didn't he? Just like he told us the shows were losing interest? Open your eyes, Sash, before it's too late!"

Without a backwards glance, Finn stomped

off towards the house. Sasha gave a deep sigh of frustration.

★

Alice was still thinking about Sasha and Finn's argument as they travelled home. Turning off the main road, Josephine indicated towards the village of Brockley, home of Park Farm.

Her mum frowned, breaking the silence. "Marcus certainly had some interesting things to say about Finn."

"I don't trust Marcus at all!" Alice responded hotly. "Finn's brilliant – look what he's done with Archie and Coco."

Josephine peered at her closely, and Alice willed herself to look neutral.

"Well, I wasn't at all taken with that Marcus chap," her mum said firmly. "Finn's a talented rider, and I need someone like him. But, Alice, I think it's best you keep your distance, don't you?

We've got a busy season and I don't want you getting distracted."

Alice sighed. Maybe her mum was right: perhaps it was best not to get involved. But deep down she knew she *was* involved. She was completely drawn into Finn's world now.

Chapter 11

The next couple of weeks were so busy with shows, lessons and schooling sessions that Alice barely had time to think. She tried to carry on with her work on Secret, with mixed results. It was so frustrating; she was positive he was capable of so much, but just when Alice thought she'd had a breakthrough he'd rebel.

One particularly awful session lodged in Alice's

mind. Aware that Finn was over, and determined to show him what she and Secret could do, she had perfected a beautiful trot across the diagonal, and was feeling rather smug. Finn glanced over at her, and Alice was sure he looked impressed.

She decided to push it and ask for an extension. She really wanted to hold Finn's attention. But Secret had other ideas and ground to a halt, yawning and pawing the ground. It was a hot day and Alice could tell he wanted to go and splash in the water trough with Tudor.

Alice was suddenly aware of Finn shouting at her and frantically making some sort of gesture and, before she could stop him, Secret buckled his knees and flopped down to roll. Alice only just managed to jump clear in time and haul him up. Shaking like a big dog, Secret gleefully dragged Alice all the way back to the stable yard, whinnying excitedly for his friends. There was no way Alice

could stop him as he was too strong. Burning with embarrassment, Alice quickly untacked Secret, hoping to get him back into his field and run into the house as quickly as possible.

No such luck.

Finn appeared, looking very amused. "You know Sasha could teach you how to make a pony lie down on command, if you wanted. Though I'm not sure what all those prissy showing judges would say."

"Ha ha," Alice replied icily.

"In all seriousness," Finn continued, "have you tried riding him away from the arena with no agenda and no training? And just enjoyed being with him?"

Alice decided to ignore Finn. Secret gave a sigh and rested his head adoringly on her shoulder, breathing his sweet warm breath in her ear. Alice held her head up high, trying to think cool and serene thoughts as she untied him. Finn looked at her, studying her face closely. He started to say something but Alice pushed past him as she led Secret back into his paddock. It was only later, when Alice glanced at the mirror in the hallway, that she realised Secret's snuffling had left a trail of green and white froth all over one cheek and in her hair. That must have been what Finn was about to tell her. She quickly wiped it off, glaring at her reflection. It couldn't get any worse!

★

Alice still wasn't completely sure if her mum had believed Marcus when he'd said Finn was a troublemaker. Josephine was always quite cool with Finn, but he had definitely impressed her with his riding as she had put his name down on the entry forms for the rest of the show season.

Alice always found herself hanging around the

yard when Finn was there, pretending to do other stuff. Aware of her mum's disapproval she tried to watch from a distance, hiding in places like the top of the hayloft, which overlooked the arena, when she couldn't think of an imaginary job to do in the yard.

"What on earth are you doing?" Fergus asked one morning as he climbed the ladder into the loft.

Alice jumped. She hadn't expected anyone to come up, and felt a blush rising to her cheeks. "Nothing." She tried to sound casual. "Counting ... hay bales."

Fergus peered through the grubby window into the arena below where Finn was cantering a beautiful circle. He chuckled. "Spying, were we?"

"No!" Alice said crossly, a bit too quickly and then she sighed. "I'm just trying to work out how he does what he does."

"He's got what my dad used to call proper horse sense," Fergus said wisely. "You're either born with it, or you're not, I guess."

Alice turned back to the window as they continued to watch Finn's schooling, digesting Fergus's words. What if she wasn't born with it? Was that why she was failing with Secret?

★

One hot afternoon, as they loaded a couple of ponies back up after lessons at Finn's yard, Marcus strolled over to the horsebox. Finn tensed as his teammate leaned casually against the side of the lorry. Even though Marcus was very handsome, Alice thought he just looked mean.

"Amazed you've still got time for the Fillies," he drawled as Finn unzipped his riding boots. "Talk about no dedication."

Alice frowned, remembering the way Marcus had practically begged her mum to offer Finn extra

hours. But her mum was out of earshot now.

"Of course I do!" Finn snapped in reply.

Marcus raised an eyebrow.

"I mean it," Finn continued angrily. "The team always comes first."

"You know, I don't know why your sister bothers," Marcus snapped. "She only stays here for you, and now you go off and find some other job."

"That's not true," Finn spat out. "Sasha's happy for me to do this. At least I'm trying to help her by earning a bit of money. More than can be said for you. I *know* you're out to destroy the team."

"You don't know anything of the sort," Marcus hissed. He stepped forward, but seeing Alice next to Finn he stopped and laughed instead. "Sasha always says you have an excellent imagination."

And with that Marcus pushed his mirrored sunglasses down over his eyes and wandered off. Jack, one of the Dales ponies, eagerly thrust his nose towards him as he passed. But Marcus swatted him away as if he was no more than an annoying fly.

★

A few days later Alice and Fergus had just finished bathing the ponies, so they looked their best for the next day's show. As well as Archie and Dolly, a lovely Welsh Section B pony, they were also taking Secret, and Alice was already dreading it. Secret was watching them with interest from his stable, managing to look so naughty and innocent all at once that Alice blew him a kiss. She thought about the one and only time she had attempted to bathe Secret on her own. He had untied himself, snapped the hose connector in two and trotted around the yard with his mane full of bubbles, a gleeful look in his eyes. It had taken three people and a bucket of feed to catch him, and Alice

hadn't tried it again.

"Oh, I nearly didn't tell you!" Fergus said, leaning on his broom. "Do you remember that mare we dropped off for Finn and Sasha?"

"Of course," said Alice, squinting up at him.

"Well, Marcus paid my brother a visit." He frowned. "Something about sending off the change of ownership form so the passport could be changed into *his* name. He told my brother he and Sasha were business partners, but I didn't think they were, did you? And Sasha had already completed all the paperwork in her name. Don't you think that's a bit strange?"

Alice frowned, before shrugging. It *was* strange. She thought Sasha had said she'd paid for the pony. But if Marcus completed the owner's documents in his name, then legally the Highland would belong to him. But Marcus *was* Sasha's boyfriend, and a member of the Flying Fillies team, so perhaps that was just how they ran things.

They were interrupted by Alice's mum who was in show-preparation mode, marching around the yard ticking items off her list. Alice sighed. Her mum seemed extra stressed about tomorrow, and Alice could only guess it was because Archie's wealthy owner was coming to watch.

Josephine swept into the wash box, running her hands through non-existent tangles in Dolly's silken tail. "Right. All set? Samantha is coming tomorrow so you need to be *extra* nice, Alice."

Alice turned to Fergus once Josephine had left to go and boss Shelley about. "What did Mum mean by that?" she said, wrinkling her nose.

Fergus shrugged. "Samantha's an important client," he said. "Your mum wants to keep her on side. She's wealthy and apparently she wants to get a few more ponies."

Alice made a face. It was always about the

business, and the money. No wonder Finn was kept firmly at a distance; despite being super horsey he and Sasha were definitely not Josephine's kind of people!

99

Chapter 12

The show was being held locally, by the coast, and everyone was enjoying the sunshine. The Flying Fillies were due on later that afternoon but the ridden pony classes were before lunch. Alice scanned the lorry park to see if there was any sign of Finn, and her stomach flipped as she saw him approaching. She noticed several girls turn round as he passed them, but he completely ignored their hair flicking

and giggling. He looked very smart, wearing a shirt and tie with a tweed jacket slung over his shoulder and his worn boots freshly polished.

"Hi," Alice said. Before she could stop herself she flicked her hair over her shoulder too, in what she imagined was a cool and relaxed manner. Because her hair was so long it took a lot of flicking.

Finn just looked at her. "Have you got a fly on you?" He had a small smile on his face.

Alice looked confused. "No. Why?"

"Oh, nothing," he replied back airily. Then he properly smiled. "Glad to be here actually, after the morning I've had." He told Alice how Sasha and Marcus had had a huge fight.

"What about?" Alice asked curiously.

Finn looked around, as if he expected Marcus to pop up from behind the horsebox.

"Honestly, I think Sasha might be seeing sense at last," he explained. "She found Marcus researching

101

the sale value of the yard online last night and it all blew up. He told her he was just '*curious*'. As if!"

Alice was about to ask him more when they were interrupted by her mum.

"Don't just stand there!" she said in an irritated voice. "There's plenty to do!"

But before she could boss Alice and Finn around further an excited voice rang through the crowd. "Josie, yoo-hoo!"

Everyone turned to look as a lady dressed in white jeans and gold sandals approached. She was carrying the tiniest dog Alice had ever seen.

"That's Samantha," her mum hissed, poking Alice on the arm.

Then, like a switch, Alice's mum turned on her brightest smile, and leapt forward.

"Samantha, how wonderful to see you!" she cooed, waving at the woman to come and join them. "Look how beautiful your outfit is, and what

a dear little dog!"

For a split second, Alice's eyes met Finn's. Alice desperately wanted to tell him that she knew how unfair it was for her mum to only turn on the charm when it suited her, but Finn had already turned back to Archie, shaking his head in bemusement.

Smiling happily, Samantha kissed Alice's mum on both cheeks. She was really elegant, with a deep tan and very blonde hair. As Samantha turned to her, Alice was struck by the warmth of Samantha's smile.

"You must be Alice!"

Before Alice knew it she found herself enveloped in a hug. Samantha's perfume was sweet and expensive-smelling and tickled her nose, a strange scent among the hay and warm ponies and tack.

"And this must be Secret!" Samantha continued, admiring the little roan who was craning his neck to give Samantha's dog a friendly sniff. "I've heard all about him. How he was born in a flood and fell in a ditch, and how his last owner gave him to you. How wonderful! It's like a pony book!" She clapped her hands together, looking delighted.

Alice was amazed. She couldn't remember *any* of her mum's clients ever taking an interest in her own pony. She decided she liked Samantha a lot.

"And there's my Archie – sweet boy!" Samantha dropped a flurry of kisses on to the pony's nose, much to his and Finn's bemusement. "Oh, he's looking so good Josie!"

Alice noticed Finn raise an eyebrow at this; no one called her mum Josie and she always corrected them if they did. But in Samantha's case her mum just smiled indulgently.

"I love ponies so much," Samantha said. "I always wanted one as a little girl, and now here I am!" She grinned at Finn. "And I hear you've done a great job riding Archie!"

Finn shrugged. "It's easy – he's a quality pony," he said simply.

The pair won their class after another lovely show, much to Samantha's delight. Alice thought how wonderfully refreshing Samantha's excitement was. Anyone would have thought it was the Horse of the Year Show rather than a local fair from the way she jumped up and down and cheered! Samantha was so happy that it lifted the mood of the whole team.

Alice was second in a big class on Dolly, the Welsh pony she was riding. The mare had behaved beautifully and her mum seemed pleased. But now it was Secret's turn.

Alice felt sick, knowing all eyes would be on her. Not only was her mum one of the most well-known show pony producers in the country, but Secret's dam, the beautiful Lily, had won at Olympia. Alice knew everyone would want to see if Secret could do as well as her. Despite this it dawned on Alice that impressing Finn was now more important to her than impressing the other riders on the circuit.

Finn leaned on the arena fence as Alice warmed up. Secret was bright and happy and seemed quite cooperative. Maybe, just maybe, they would do well…

"He's not going to try his new trick is he?" Finn grinned, referring to Secret's attempted roll a few days ago.

"Oh, shut up!" Alice's nerves made her snappy as she entered the ring.

Almost immediately Secret seemed to lose his sparkle, exactly as he had at the country fair. Frowning, Alice gave him a scratch on his withers. After a few laps of the ring she started to worry he might be ill, but she pressed on, shaking any doubt from her mind. She *had* to do well. The judge called the pair into a provisional first place and her mum

gave Alice a thumbs-up from the ringside. All they had to do was a good individual show, and the red rosette was theirs. Secret *really* didn't feel right though. Alice had to work hard to encourage him forward in front of the judge, a stern-looking lady in a navy suit. She nodded briskly as Alice said a polite good morning.

After walking round Secret, hands behind her back, the judge indicated for Alice to start. Alice nudged Secret forward and … nothing. Her heart sank. Not now, not here! Nudging him again slightly harder, colour starting to rise to her cheeks, Alice began to silently plead. Instead Secret calmly stretched himself out and gave a long relieved sigh. Alice realised with horror that Secret was having the longest wee in history, accompanied by a low groan of relief. Even worse, the ground was so dry that the wee wasn't sinking in, but was instead running over the dusty earth like some terrible stream, and the judge had to neatly sidestep to avoid her shoes from getting ruined.

Aware of a ripple of laughter from the ringside and, imagining Finn joining in, Alice was mortified. She completely lost her composure, so much so that when Secret had finished he took full advantage of Alice's lapse in concentration and trotted straight out of the arena. This meant instant dismissal from the class.

"What was that? Why did you let him just trot off like that?" Her mum sounded horrified as she caught the little roan.

"Sorry."

There was nothing more Alice could say. She had totally messed this one up. But it wasn't just the fact that Secret had had a wee; it was something else, something bigger. It suddenly dawned on Alice that perhaps Secret hated showing as much as she did!

Chapter 13

As Alice walked Secret back to the horsebox Finn caught up with her. "Hey!"

Alice was too miserable to be snappy with Finn. Her performance was a stark reminder that she was not as good a rider as him.

"Don't tell me, how did I get him to do that, what a good trick, oh, why don't I train my pony better, blah blah blah," Alice muttered.

Finn looked sideways at her, giving Secret a pat. "Actually I thought you rode him beautifully in the warm-up … before the pit stop."

Alice looked at him in surprise. She hadn't expected him to praise her.

"Really?" she said uncertainly.

"Yes, really," Finn said. "But, Alice, haven't you thought that showing might not be right for Secret? I mean, I haven't seen that much of him really, but I just have a feeling it's not for him. Or for you," he added after a pause.

Alice thought of her dreams of cantering Secret on a beach or jumping fallen trees, and her love of riding cross-country on Honey before her fall. The show ring didn't feature in her dreams at all. She knew Finn was right.

"You try talking to Mum," she replied sulkily. "I'd love to do pony club, or showjumping, but I can't, can I? I never have time. It's not like I can

just do whatever I want, like you."

Finn fixed her with a level gaze. "At least your mum cares," he said softly, and Alice was reminded about his dad taking off around the world after his mum had died. Finn never really mentioned him, but it had to be hard. She fell silent, feeling ashamed. There she was moaning about pony club rallies, and Finn had effectively lost both his mum *and* his dad.

As they neared the box, they could hear Samantha talking excitedly to Josephine about new ponies. Archie and Dolly were dozing in the shade and Samantha had laid out the most amazing picnic on a fold-out table. There was smoked salmon, open sandwiches topped with mozzarella and tomatoes, a fruit salad and cupcakes decorated with horseshoes.

Samantha beckoned over the teenagers once Alice had got Secret settled with a hay net.

"Please, help yourself!" she said happily. "Finn, you were amazing with Archie! I can't wait for my girls to ride him. They would have been here today, but they're at tennis camp."

"I'd love to, but I can't eat anything now," Finn said. "I have to go and get ready for the display."

"That sounds marvellous!" Samantha cried excitedly. "Oh, Alice, let's go and watch him!"

Alice knew she needed to go home with her mum and help with the ponies, but she longed to watch Finn's display again and spend more time with Samantha. Plus she was keen to avoid her mum after Secret's class! Her mum wouldn't say anything now in front of Samantha, but she would at home. Alice needed some time to think about what had happened today with Secret, and how Finn's thoughts had mirrored her own.

"I'll drop Alice home," Samantha continued, addressing Alice's mum, "and then perhaps you

and I can have a chat, Josie? I've seen a lovely Connemara for sale that I hoped you might take on?"

Alice knew her mum would be overjoyed at this. Smiling, Josephine agreed that she would take the ponies back home and Alice could stay with Samantha to watch the Flying Fillies. Alice felt her excitement grow. It was rare she had a break.

Her mum wasn't going to let Alice get away easily though. While Samantha took a phone call, she cornered Alice next to the horsebox ramp. "Alice, you do remember what I said, don't you?" She looked straight at her. "Finn's a great rider, and I know Samantha likes him, but I'd prefer if you didn't get too involved."

Alice crossed her arms over her chest. "Why, Mum?" However well Finn rode the ponies, her mum still didn't seem to like him and it just wasn't fair.

Josephine raised an eyebrow. "Come on, Alice, there's lots of issues there; you must be able to see that. I don't much like Marcus, but what if there *is* something dodgy going on with Finn?"

"Well, actually," Alice replied defiantly, "I think *Marcus* is the one who's trouble. I think you haven't ever given Finn a real chance, or bothered to get to know him. If you had, you'd see what I see. Just because he's not like you, not like any of this!" She gestured around at the showground.

"Oh, Alice." Josephine sighed in a way that suggested mums are always right, and started to load the ponies in the horsebox.

★

Once Josephine had left, Alice and Samantha strolled arm in arm to the main ring, where the showjumping was drawing to a close. Settling down on the grass, they waited for the ring to clear, watching the helpers scurrying around,

dismantling the jumps.

"So, what's going on with you and Finn?" Samantha asked Alice.

"What do you mean?" Alice tried to sound casual.

Samantha laughed kindly. "Oh, I just have a feeling!" Looking at her warm, smiling face, Alice wanted to open up, but she wasn't sure what to say.

"Nothing … really," she said instead. "I guess we're friends…"

Before Samantha could ask anything else, the familiar drum roll sounded the start of the display and Sasha galloped in on her big grey horse, her blonde hair covered by the hood of a scarlet cloak that billowed out behind her. There were some gasps of admiration as Sasha and her horse performed their trademark rear. Next was Molly, standing across the backs of the pair of Dales. Then came Marcus. The girls in the crowd giggled as Marcus cantered past but Alice noticed he wasn't smirking as normal. He just looked a bit bored, as if he was going through the motions. Then Finn entered the ring in his black outfit, Horatio performing a breathtaking extended trot, feathers and mane flying.

"Oh, wonderful!" Samantha cried, clearly delighted, as her little dog yapped its approval.

Alice never grew tired of watching the ponies gallop across the arena, the riders performing all manner of tricks, but as Sasha cantered past Alice looked closely at her. She was smiling, but it looked fixed. Perhaps she was still upset after her row with Marcus about the price of the yard, but suddenly Alice had a dark sense of foreboding.

Finn was galloping across the arena, throwing himself as far over the saddle as possible so that he was almost upside down. Molly crossed him in

the centre, perfectly balanced on the back of the two Dales ponies. Waving to the cheering crowd, Molly slowed her ponies as Sasha's grey thundered down the middle for the highlight of the display.

As her horse slowed, Sasha climbed into a standing position. In one fluid motion she was balancing on one leg, the other stretched out behind her in a perfect ballerina pose. The crowd went wild. Just for a second Alice noticed a look of panic cross Sasha's face, and then she watched in horror as, almost in slow motion, the girth securing the simple saddle sprang open and Sasha started to slip. Panicked by the sudden movement on his back, the big grey spooked, dislodging Sasha who crashed on to his neck before falling heavily to the ground with a sickening thud. Her horse bolted and the crowd, realising it wasn't part of the act, gasped as Sasha lay motionless on the grass.

Chapter 14

Alice and Samantha jumped to their feet as Finn thundered past, leaping off Horatio and sprinting to where Sasha lay. Marcus was trying to control his horse and Molly was attempting to climb down from her ponies as Sasha's grey circled the arena. He was calmer and had slowed to a trot but was in danger of standing on his trailing reins. Without thinking, Alice vaulted over the arena barriers.

Sasha's horse wasn't difficult to catch and Alice was soon leading him over to Finn's pony. She took hold of his reins, too. Finn was kneeling on the floor next to Sasha, and Marcus had finally calmed his horse enough to approach them. To Alice's relief, as the ambulance roared into the arena Sasha climbed groggily to her feet, only to be firmly told off by the paramedics.

Marcus was closely studying the saddle. "Didn't anyone check the girth?" he said, frowning at Finn.

"We both did." Finn was pale-faced as Sasha was placed on to a stretcher. "I always check it at least twice." He shook his head, totally distraught.

Going cold, Alice remembered what he had said weeks ago, about the tack needing replacing.

Sasha was protesting that she was fine. "Look after my horse, and Finn, stay here, make sure the ponies get home safe," she pleaded as she was carried away. Her horse whickered after her, his eyes full of concern.

"Thanks, Alice." Finn took hold of Horatio's reins from her, looking shaken. "The girth must have just snapped. I can't believe I didn't notice."

"It's not your fault, Finn," Sasha called after him as she was loaded into the ambulance. "I mended it a few days ago. I should have just chucked it out!"

The ambulance made its way steadily out of the ring. A few onlookers gawped in morbid curiosity but mostly the spectators had drifted away.

"Well, we may as well call it a day," Marcus said casually, heading for the arena exit.

Alice thought that Marcus didn't seem particularly bothered about what had happened. She remembered how bored he had appeared when he first rode in. She *really* disliked Marcus!

Still clutching the grey's reins, Alice started to follow the remaining team back to their lorry as

Samantha joined them.

"Anything I can do?" she asked, as Finn stared through her. He looked really shocked, Alice thought.

"I-I need to be with Sasha." He stumbled over his words, but Samantha seemed to understand straight away.

"I'll take you to see her," she said reassuringly. "I'll drop Alice home, and come and collect you, give you a chance to get your ponies settled. That OK?"

Finn nodded and Alice decided Samantha had to be one of the kindest people she had ever met.

★

Once she and Samantha had helped Finn load up the horses for their journey home, Alice climbed into Samantha's four-by-four. Samantha was silent as they pulled out of the showground. As she indicated off the main road she finally spoke.

★

★
★
121
★

"He's a good kid, Finn. I think he's a bit lost underneath all that attitude. That display was the most amazing thing I've ever seen. I can't wait to show my girls. Such talent!"

Alice stared out of the window at the fields whizzing by, thinking about what Samantha had said. It was such a contrast to how her mum saw Finn. The air was thick with dust as combines chugged up and down the crops. Although it was the height of summer, there was the faintest hint of autumn round the corner. Alice knew that Finn and Sasha needed the income from the final few shows of the summer holidays, or they faced a long, hard winter. She crossed her fingers, hoping Sasha was going to be OK. Samantha's words had struck a chord with her too. *He's a bit lost*. She had seen something very vulnerable in Finn today and she couldn't stop thinking about him.

★

★
★ ★

"All OK?" Josephine was engrossed in paperwork and barely looked up as Alice came in. Ignoring her mum and hopping over Poppy, Alice raced up the stairs to her bedroom.

A moment later there was a knock on the door and then her mum appeared. "Al?" she asked gently, and Alice looked up from where she was sitting on the bed. Taking in her pale face, her mum sat down next to her.

"Oh, Mum," Alice said. Then she poured out the story of Sasha's fall, as Josephine listened quietly. Alice was grateful she didn't bring up the subject of Secret's performance.

"Where's Finn now?" her mum asked once Alice had finished.

"Went back to do his ponies," Alice said miserably.

Nodding, Josephine stood up, reaching for her mobile phone. "I'll give him a call and check up on him," she said, to Alice's surprise. "I knew that sort of riding was ridiculous! He should stick to the show ring."

Alice just looked at her. Finn, like Secret, didn't belong in the show ring.

"Not everyone wants to do what you do, Mum," she muttered.

★

Later, once she had had a shower, Alice wandered down to the yard, her damp hair drying quickly in the late-afternoon sunshine. She needed to be near Secret. Her mum had gone back out for the afternoon to judge at another show and both Shelley and Fergus were out. Only her dad was around, and he was in his study. Alice's only job was to ride Lachlan, something her mum trusted her to do on her own. She wondered if her mum had managed to speak to Finn.

Secret was back in his stable, dozing in the cool.

A PONY called SECRET

Alice stared at him over the door, thinking again about what Finn had said.

"What do you think, boy?" She cupped her hands out towards Secret as he bustled over. "Are you cut out for something else?"

"Talking to yourself again?"

The familiar voice made Alice spin round and Secret whicker. It was Finn, standing in the entrance to the barn, his dog, Lima, by his feet.

"Finn!" Alice gasped. "What are you doing here…? How's Sasha?"

Finn gave a small smile. "Well, firstly, Samantha brought me back, and, secondly, Sasha's OK. She's sprained her ankle badly, but nothing is broken and the doctors say she'll be able to ride again soon as long as she's careful. So I think we'll be OK to do the last few shows."

"That's great news!" Alice said, relieved.

A frown crossed Finn's face. "Yeah," he agreed.

"The girth just snapped. I knew it was worn, but I didn't realise how much. It could have been so much worse... If she had fallen a bit to the left..." His voice trailed off, and Alice shuddered, remembering how close Sasha had come to being trampled.

Finn shook his head, then continued. "Your mum rang and said I could stay here for the night, in the groom's flat with Fergus. Sasha's staying in hospital until tomorrow and I didn't want to be at home by myself." He scuffed his worn boots in the dust.

That was really nice of Mum, Alice thought, pleased.

"Were the ponies OK?" she asked.

Finn smiled. "Samantha helped me turn them all out, before we went to hospital," he said. "She's really nice, wants me to ride all her ponies when she sends them here."

So he's going to be around a lot more, Alice thought happily, trying not to look too pleased.

They were both silent for a minute as they watched Secret, who was back at his hay net, eating with huge enthusiasm, dragging each mouthful through his water bucket. He really was the messiest pony on the yard!

"Anyway," Finn said, stretching, "I need to keep my mind off things. Why don't we hack out?"

"What, now?" Alice said, startled. "Just us?"

Finn looked around. "Well, I don't see anyone else, do you?"

"It's just … I normally go with Fergus," Alice said nervously. Although Josephine was keen that all the ponies were hacked out regularly, they were always very routine with Fergus leading a pony and Alice trotting behind.

Finn shrugged. "So?"

"I *do* need to ride Lachlan…" Alice said slowly.

127

"Perfect. I'll ride Lachie, you take Secret," Finn said.

Nodding, Alice agreed, and before she knew it she and Finn were clattering out of the gates on the two ponies. She felt as if she was skipping school! Secret, who adored going out, pricked his ears, jogging besides Lachlan.

"Where do you normally go?" Finn was relaxed, reins in one hand.

"Um … take a left, round the village and back up the long hill to the yard."

Finn made a face. "Boring. What about going this way?"

He indicated a bridleway that led on to the downs. Alice had walked there often enough with Poppy. Before she could stop him Finn had swung the gate open, grinning at her to follow him. After a moment's hesitation Alice nudged Secret on, and the little pony followed, free and easy, with

no hint of any naughtiness. It didn't take long for the bridleway to open up into an inviting expanse of rolling ground. As Finn urged Lachlan into a canter, Alice did the same, and just for a few minutes, as their shadows stretched out long in front of them and the ponies' manes flew behind them, Alice felt free for the first time since her accident. This was what she had waited for over four years to do: just ride her pony, with nothing to worry about!

"Come on!" Finn laughed over his shoulder as they slowed back to a trot. "Look ahead!"

Alice looked. There was the most inviting mossy log lying in their path, only about half a metre high, the sort of thing Alice used to adore jumping on Honey.

"I'll check it out." Riding ahead, Finn gave Lachlan a pat as he surveyed the landing side of the log. It was perfect ground, with no holes or hazards. "Why not?" he said with a grin, going back to Alice.

Alice took a deep breath, realising she wasn't even nervous. She wanted to jump the log more than anything and she felt Secret did as well. She nudged Secret forward. Ears pricked, soft and responsive, Secret broke into a rolling canter. There was no hint of the bored pony Alice had grown used to. Although the log was only tiny, the rush of happiness was huge as Secret sailed the jump, landing in a controlled canter.

Half an hour later, as they cooled the ponies down on their walk home, Alice didn't think she would stop smiling.

"How about that then, Alice in her palace?" Finn grinned as they turned into the lane towards the yard. "That's the best I've seen you look together. Imagine the future, if you could do that?"

Alice ignored the dreaded nickname. The ride

had been amazing. Secret had felt his very best: alive, spirited and free, but working with her in a partnership. Her mind was now made up. Secret didn't belong in the show ring. He had been trying to tell her for years, and she had only just realised.

★

With Samantha in no hurry to get home, and Finn staying with Fergus for the night, an impromptu supper was laid on in the kitchen. Everyone helped themselves from the plates of food piled on the big wooden table, talking happily about ponies, pony shows and more ponies.

Alice asked Finn if he had heard from Sasha. He nodded, pulling out his mobile.

"She texted me to say she was OK. One of the nurses has got her *Horse and Hound* to read," he said, looking at the message on the screen.

"Is Marcus with her?" Alice asked, and Finn looked angry.

"He turned up after I left," he said. "Probably trying to get back into her good books after their fight this morning." Running a hand through his hair, still full of dust from the show, Finn frowned. "He's definitely up to something. Why else would he be seeing how much the yard is worth? Surely she's *got* to see sense now…"

Chapter 15

A few days later, Alice and Fergus went over to Rookham Manor to drop off Archie and the new Connemara, Merlin, for Finn to ride.

"Hello?" Fergus called as he opened the tack-room door. Sasha was slumped on a pile of rugs in the corner, head in hands, face streaked with tears. Finn was pacing back and forth, his expression a mix of worry and fury. Alice frowned as she noticed

Marcus leaning against a pile of rugs, playing with his phone and looking bored.

"Um…" Fergus pushed the door a little wider. "All OK?"

"No," Finn said. His voice was so icy that a shiver went down Alice's spine.

Fergus tried again. "Is there anything we can do to help?"

"Only if you can ring all of the shows and convince them to book us," Finn said bitterly as Sasha started to cry again.

"I just don't understand!" she sobbed. "We've never had a problem, and now they've all cancelled on us!"

"What's this about?" Alice asked Finn quietly.

He pressed a hand against his tanned forehead. "The last shows have all cancelled," he said, glaring at Marcus. "*Apparently.*"

"I told you, Finn," Marcus said with a yawn.

"They all rang while Sasha was in hospital, and you were gallivanting around at the posh show yard. They said they were terribly sorry but they'd heard about the fall and they'd rather book something else, something more *reliable*, because, let's face it, the last show was a disaster."

"I just can't believe they *all* thought that!" Finn sounded desperate.

"Oh, Finn." Marcus's tone was patronising. "I'm as disappointed as you. All that work booking them in the first place. *Such* a shame." He shook his head, not looking at all disappointed. "We've got to think of a plan for the winter, Sash."

"What plan? To try to get Sasha to sell this place?" Finn had his fists balled now. "Have you explained to her why you were looking up the price of the yard?"

"Sasha knows everything I do is for her own good," Marcus said smugly. "She needs me!"

"You good-for-nothing piece of—" Finn swung out at Marcus, but Fergus stepped in front of him and grabbed his fist.

Sasha had been watching the whole exchange silently. "My brother's right," she said slowly to Marcus, as if it was just sinking in. "You've never tried to help us; you've been trying to break us from the start!"

"Oh come on, Sash." Marcus chuckled. "Can't you see how much better life would be if you could just get away from this place? Finn's busy with his precious job now, and the Flying Fillies are pretty much over, so what have you got to lose?"

Sasha's face flashed with fury. She threw the nearest thing she could find at Marcus, an ancient pink dandy brush. "I can't *believe* it's taken me this long to see through you!" she cried. "Just get out. Get out of the yard, and my life!"

★

★
★　　★

A PONY called SECRET

"Do you mind if we skip schooling for today?" Finn leaned wearily against Archie's side a little later. "Just ride around the fields instead?"

"OK," Alice agreed, swinging lightly up into Archie's saddle. Mounting Merlin, Finn clattered out of the yard and, reaching down, fiddled with the catch on a gate, pushing it open. A rotten piece of rail collapsed next to it, tumbling to the overgrown grass.

"Well, that's just perfect!" Finn exploded, before patting Merlin. "I'm sorry, boy, I didn't mean to startle you." Then he gave Alice a crooked smile. "Or you, Alice." There was something about the way he looked at her that made Alice drop her gaze first.

They rode side by side, the ponies relaxed and stretching their heads long and low, and Alice felt brave enough to ask Finn what he and Sasha were going to do now.

Finn held his head high. "What we've always done. Start again, work hard and get the Flying Fillies going once more, *without* Marcus. Sasha loves this yard, and so do I. We'd never *ever* sell it, and I can't believe Marcus even thought she would consider it!"

But however fiercely he said the words, Alice noticed a slight quaver to his voice. Finn's future looked very uncertain.

★

As the teenagers completed their loop of the parkland, Finn told Alice a little more about his dad, who was currently working in Andalusia, Spain.

Although she didn't want to say it, the more Finn told her, the more Alice thought how selfish his dad sounded. "If he knew about the shows being cancelled," she asked thoughtfully, "would he come back to help?"

Finn shook his head. "Sasha still won't tell him," he said, sighing. "I wish she would. She thinks he has enough on his mind. She says if we can just get over this and secure some new bookings, then we can scrape by."

"Oh." Alice knew how lucky she was. Josephine might be completely obsessed with showing, but Alice never needed to worry about paying the vet's bills or feed bills. And, most importantly, she had both her parents around. It was funny, she thought; she envied Finn's freedom, and yet he envied her security. The ponies really were the only common ground they had.

Samantha's ponies were calm, and as they walked along on a loose rein Alice found herself talking to Finn about things she never told anyone. About her accident with Honey and the day she had been released from hospital, to meeting Secret for the first time. Finn really listened to her. He didn't tease her, or call her 'Alice in her palace'. They chatted about the other ponies on the yard, including Lachlan, who it turned out was related to the mare Fergus and Alice had delivered all those weeks ago.

Finn looked thoughtful. "I'm pretty sure they're half siblings. Remind me to dig out her passport when we get back, so I can check."

"What did you call her in the end?" Alice asked.

"Sasha named her Hope." Finn clucked at Merlin as they headed for home. "Which is exactly what we need right now."

★

The sun was high in the sky when Alice and Finn returned from the hack, and they busied themselves sponging the hot ponies down and filling hay nets. There was no sign of Fergus or Sasha.

Finn clicked his fingers. "Oh yes, Hope's passport. Come with me."

A PONY called SECRET

Following Finn across the yard into the cool of the kitchen, Alice tried not to stare. It was the first time she had been in the house. Although shabby, it was beautiful. There were mementos of Finn's dad's nomadic life everywhere, polo sticks propped up in the corner, a western saddlecloth draped over the sofa where a cat blinked sleepily up at them. Finn's dog was lying on the flagstones, and thumped his wiry tail sleepily as they walked in.

Finn bent down to stroke the dog, who stretched luxuriously. "Good boy, Lima."

"That's a funny name for a dog," Alice remarked. She was studying South America in geography. "It's the capital of Peru."

"I know." Finn chuckled. "Dad found him wandering around the streets there as a puppy and paid a fortune to get him home."

It was easy to see where Finn got his love of

horses and dogs from. Maybe like Finn, his dad was better with animals than people.

Like Alice's kitchen, there were photos of horses everywhere. Ponies in the show ring ridden by a younger Sasha, and Finn being led around on an enormous Friesian by a dark-haired man. Alice spotted a photo of a woman who looked exactly like Sasha riding a big grey side-saddle, throwing her head back and laughing. She looked so happy. It had to be Finn's mum. For just a second Alice felt Finn's pain as if she had been punched in the stomach, and it nearly took her breath away.

Finn was rifling through papers on a desk, looking confused. "That's weird," he muttered.

"What's up?" Alice asked.

"The pony passports!" Finn exclaimed. "They're all missing!"

Scratching his head, he looked around. "I wonder if we left them in the lorry, after all the

drama when Sash fell."

But the passports weren't in the lorry either. Alice could tell Finn was getting worried. Sasha hobbled across the yard, her face still puffy from crying.

She frowned as Finn asked her about the missing passports. "Are they not in the desk? The horsebox then?" she questioned as Finn shook his head.

"No." He sounded agitated. "I've looked. They've gone!"

Sasha shook her head angrily. "Finn, they cost hundreds of pounds to replace! How can they be *missing*? I always put them back as soon as we get home from a show! Why didn't you? You know they're important!"

"I was a little preoccupied after you fell," Finn said icily. "Don't blame me!"

"Great." Sasha threw her hands up. "I mean, that's all we need, isn't it?"

As the siblings argued, Alice frowned. Why did this seem familiar? When Fergus returned, ready to give her a lift back home, Finn barely noticed as she climbed into the cab, as he and Sasha continued to squabble.

Chapter 16

Over the next couple of weeks Alice saw a lot of Finn. Samantha added a pretty Exmoor mare to her growing herd, and she wanted Finn to ride all her ponies. Sasha was back on her feet again, practising her moves on her grey horse. Finn had told Alice they were spending every evening trying to drum up business, but that Sasha had taken a waitressing job to tide them over.

Alice had been around Rookham Manor long enough now to know Finn and Sasha still had money problems. She had been relieved when Finn had told her that the next-door farmer had cut their hay for them for virtually nothing, so at least the ponies' winter fodder was sorted. It made Alice really happy to see the hay stacked up next to the tack room, ready to go up into the loft. The sight of the sweet meadow hay was reassuring!

According to Finn, Sasha and Marcus were now completely over. So it took Alice by surprise when Marcus appeared one morning at Rookham Manor with a tall blond man. There was something about the way the man peered around the yard, cigarette dangling from his lips, that sent shivers down Alice's spine.

She was sitting on the mounting block, watching as Finn rode Merlin in the front paddock. Seeing the two men, Finn urged Merlin into a canter and

clattered into the yard.

"What do you want, Marcus?" Finn practically spat. "Sasha's not here."

Marcus glowered at Finn. "There's stuff here that belongs to me."

Finn stood his ground. "I don't think so. This is OUR home and OUR business."

Marcus moved closer. "You can't exactly call yourself a business," he taunted. "No bookings, no money – pathetic. And to think *I* put so much time and effort into this place. Your sister owes me!"

"She owes you nothing. You're totally full of it," Finn said, his eyes flashing. "Get out, Marcus."

"Gladly, but this won't be the last you'll see of me," Marcus replied, and sauntering back down the drive he pointed and muttered something to his friend. They laughed, an unpleasant sound.

Alice stood up. "You OK?" She took Merlin's reins from Finn.

"I am now he's gone," he said furiously.

"It sounded like he was threatening you…" Alice's voice trailed off. "Do you think we need to tell someone?"

"He's completely spineless; he won't do anything," Finn replied confidently. "And what *can* he do? Sasha fired him."

Then, removing his riding hat and shaking out his damp hair, Finn burst into unexpected laughter. Alice looked at him, bemused. She'd never really heard him laugh properly before.

"We'll be OK," Finn said, once his chuckles had subsided. Then, looking around the beautiful yard, he added, "We can start over again. We're made of strong stuff!"

★

Archie was turning out to be the star of the season. Finn had qualified him for an end-of-season championship show, much to Samantha's delight.

Alice's mum was having to juggle things to make sure Finn had plenty of time to ride him.

"Hmmm," Josephine said, looking at her full diary as she planned riding time for Finn. "I'm judging a show an hour away from Finn and Sasha's place on Thursday," she continued. "If I drop Archie at Rookham Manor on my way, and then go on to judge the evening performance, I wonder if Finn would be happy to give Archie a quick training session in one of his paddocks."

"I don't see why not." Alice was sitting in Poppy's basket, her arms round the sleeping dog. Then she had a brainwave, remembering her recent ride with Finn. "Actually, Mum, can we take Secret to Finn's as well? It would be good to ride him somewhere else, for experience." She crossed her fingers as she said this, hoping Finn would suggest hacking out in the beautiful grounds surrounding his home.

"Good idea, Alice." Josephine sounded pleased. "I'll ring Sasha now. Talking of Secret, why don't we take him to a little practice show with Archie? In a couple of weeks?"

Alice fiddled with the tag on Poppy's collar. "Maybe," she said, avoiding her mum's eyes.

"OK, let's decide nearer the time." Josephine turned back to her diary, her mind on Archie. "But, Alice, we do need to talk about Secret. It's clear you're having some problems as a partnership."

Alice mumbled a reply. Until she got her thoughts straight in her head that was one conversation she wanted to avoid for now.

★

"I'll pick you up later this evening, OK?"

Alice gave her mum a quick kiss on the cheek. In her cream jacket and skirt and matching hat, she looked the picture of elegance. Archie and Secret had been unloaded into Finn and Sasha's

yard, and Josephine was on her way to judge the evening championship.

"We'll be fine, Mum. I hope it goes well tonight!"

Alice waved as she turned back towards the stables. Fergus was stepping in to help Josephine as a steward, so it was just Finn, Sasha and Alice in the yard. Alice wondered if her mum was softening towards Finn and his family at last; she couldn't have imagined being left alone at Rookham Manor at the start of the summer! And she knew Sasha was happy to have the ponies visit for an evening schooling session.

★

"When's Secret's next show?" Finn gestured at the little roan as they rode later in the front meadow. The sun was setting, throwing a fiery shade of pink over the grass, highlighting Secret's beautiful colouring.

Alice took a deep breath, her mind made up.

"I'm not doing any more showing with him."

There, she had said it. After days and days of thinking it over, Alice had finally realised what would be best for her and Secret's relationship. And as she said the words aloud she felt even more sure. She didn't want to do the next show with him; she didn't want to show him ever again.

Finn nodded in approval. "That's the best decision you've made. Does your mum know?"

Alice shook her head. "No. And she's not going to be happy."

"Why?" Finn said in surprise. "He's your pony."

"I know," Alice said, thinking about her mum's reaction. Would she be let down? Disappointed? Angry? "Oh ... it's hard to explain. It's just that she thinks he has loads of potential."

"He probably does," Finn agreed. "But it isn't what's right for you, or him. Look, I think you might be surprised at your mum. It's not like

you're giving up showing altogether, are you?"

"No!" Alice shook her head. She couldn't imagine not riding Lachlan, or Porridge, or any of the youngsters that came and went. It might not be what she truly loved, but she still wanted to help her mum.

"So, tell her then," Finn said simply. "Tell her you want to do something different with Secret, but that you'll carry on working hard with the other ponies. You're a talented rider, Alice."

Finn's compliment caught her off guard, and she glowed with pleasure. He made telling her mum sound so easy!

"So what is it that you *really* want to do with Secret?" he asked, jolting her back to the present.

Alice reached forward and gave the roan a pat. "Nothing, for a bit. Just ride him with no pressure. Start again. And then I'd really love to go back to what I did with Honey." She smiled at the memory of her faithful palomino. "Jumping. That ride I had with you, when I jumped that log, it was amazing! I could imagine me and Secret doing that. I don't think I'd jump cross-country again…" Her eyes squeezed shut as she tried to block out the painful images of Honey's accident. "But I think I'd like to showjump Secret. Though for now, I just want to enjoy being with him."

"Sounds perfect," Finn smiled. "Especially the no-pressure bit. Let's start right away. What would you like to do now?"

Alice looked around her, at the setting sun ablaze on the horizon, at the team ponies grazing peacefully in the meadows by the house, and blushed.

"I know it sounds stupid," she mumbled, "but I've always wanted to canter bareback in a meadow…" The words trailed away on her lips as Finn smiled.

"Come on then!" he laughed, jumping lightly off Archie and removing his saddle in a flash. "Let's go!"

Before she knew it Secret's saddle joined Archie's on the grass, and Alice was back on Secret, legged up by Finn. Alice's legs were so long that her feet brushed the long meadow grasses as they left the schooling area. Both ponies jigged a bit, sensing something exciting was about to happen. Following Finn, Alice rode Secret back out of the field and under a line of ancient chestnut trees. A wide, uphill meadow stretched behind the big house invitingly.

"We used to do this all the time, with Mum." Finn grinned over his shoulder. "Race you to the top!"

A surge of adrenalin flowed through Alice as Secret broke into a canter, giving a little rear of excitement as he plunged after Finn. Alice crouched low as his speed increased. As the warm breeze whipped past her and the ponies cantered to the top of the meadow side by side, she laughed out loud. This was exactly what she had dreamed of. Her and Secret, completely as one, no pressures. Why *hadn't* she done this before?

Alice was still smiling as she and Finn untacked together back in the yard. Then Sasha limped over, phone in hand.

"Your mum rang," Sasha explained. "They're running late and she's not even started judging her class yet." She made a face. "I remember all that hanging about. So she's asked if you can stay for supper with us."

Alice tried not to make it too obvious that she was over the moon to spend more time with Finn and Sasha ... especially Finn!

Sasha and Finn's horses were all out in the paddock, as they were most summer nights. But

knowing Secret's ability to find a weak spot in any fence, Alice put Archie and Secret into the old coaching stables. The stables were reached down a long cobbled corridor, and as the hoof beats echoed around the thick stone walls, Alice imagined all the horses who had walked down here over the centuries. She peeked into the tack room as she passed. It was full of extraordinary kit: ancient side-saddles, elaborate costumes and unusual bridles. Alice knew it was all used in the displays, and even though some of the objects were practically falling apart, they were totally irreplaceable.

Finn leaned on the stable door as Alice fussed over the handsome roan.

"Bet this is a shock isn't it, boy?" Finn reached over and patted Secret. "No gold-plated buckets or butlers for you here!"

Alice glared at Finn crossly. He always managed

to wind her up!

"Hardly," she said in irritation.

"All right, calm down, Alice in her palace!" Finn held his hands up, his eyes sparkling. "I was *joking.*"

Alice couldn't help chuckling as she threw a handful of hay at Finn. She finally felt like she was getting to know him, and it was a really nice feeling.

★

Supper was pizza in the garden. It was clear the garden had once been amazing, but it was more like a hayfield now. Sasha was sitting on a deckchair resting her ankle, and Finn and Alice sat on a Newmarket blanket covered with grey hairs.

"It's Robin's blanket," Sasha laughed, referring to her grey horse. "Sorry, we don't normally have guests."

"It's perfect," Alice replied, and it was. Finn and

Sasha's home may not be modern or luxurious like hers, but it was special, and romantic.

As they ate, Sasha told a few stories from her time in the show ring, and Finn chatted about Hope the Highland's progress. He was aiming for her to join the Flying Fillies next year, and it made Alice happy to hear him talk about the future in a positive way. As the evening closed in around them, they remained sitting in the garden, Finn and Alice side by side.

At nine p.m. there was still no sign of Josephine. Sasha limped back into the house to make a coffee, and Finn stretched as Lima curled into his shoulder.

"We need some rain," he remarked. "The ground is getting too hard for the…" The words died on his lips as he sat bolt upright, pressing a finger to his mouth.

"Did you hear that?" He turned to Alice, the urgency in his voice startling her. She shook her head, and Finn stood up, his eyes searching.

Sasha came back out of the house, balancing three mugs on a tray. "Here you go!" she said, making her way back towards them. Then she dropped the tray as a huge bang came from the stables.

Chapter 17

All three ran as fast as possible towards the yard, Alice's breath ragged. All she could imagine was the worst possible scenario: an explosion ... the roof falling in ... Secret trapped. As they rounded the corner into the yard the heat of a fire hit Alice, and acrid smoke filled her lungs, making her cough. The hay was ablaze, flames curling round the thick stone doorway into the tack room. For what felt like an eternity, all three stared in horror, before Sasha snapped into action.

"We need to call 999!" she screamed.

Alice was jolted to her senses, and rummaging in her pocket for her phone, threw it to Sasha and ran straight for the stables. Flames were licking the walls, growing higher, filling the walkway with smoke. A frightened whinny carried over on the still evening air, and Alice knew it came from Secret.

"No, Alice!"

Finn tried to grab Alice's arm, but she shook it off and raced forward, tearing down the corridor in the direction of the ponies. The heat was unbearable, and her eyes stung as she struggled to see in front of her. She was aware of shouting behind her, and realised Finn had followed her in.

"No!" she shouted, panicked. "Get back!" She waved frantically at Finn who had pulled his

T-shirt up over his mouth.

Finn caught up with her. "I'm not leaving you alone," he yelled. "Come on!"

Secret was pacing around his stable, his sides slick with sweat, every vein in his neck showing. Archie was at the back of his box, rolling his eyes, his whole body trembling.

"Quick, open the doors," Finn shouted. "They'll find their way out."

The crackling and popping was getting louder, and Alice cried out as Secret half reared over his stable door. She leaned against it to open it, but noticed Archie had retreated even further back, his head lowered, sides heaving violently. It was as though he was paralysed by fear. Alice realised if she let Secret go, Archie probably wouldn't follow him, and then they would have to drag him out themselves, which would be impossible.

"GO!" Finn had managed to get Archie's head

collar on and was gesturing wildly at Alice to open the door and let Secret loose. He tried to lead Archie to the stable door, but Archie flung his head up in alarm before backing up again.

"No ... wait!" Alice knew she and Secret needed to do something to help. Grabbing Secret's head collar, she made a desperate attempt to put it over his head as he thrashed around, finally managing to do up the buckle.

"Listen," she said to Finn, using all of her strength to stop Secret fleeing as she unbolted the door. "If I let Secret go, I don't think Archie will follow, and he'll be trapped. You can't move him on your own."

"Alice, GO!" Finn repeated desperately, not listening to her.

"I'm not leaving you!" Alice cried. She wasn't going to let anything happen to Archie, or Finn.

Secret was plunging about like a wild stallion,

the whites of his eyes showing. At that moment Alice knew what she needed to do. She had to put all of her trust into the little red pony, and he needed to trust her.

She placed a reassuring hand on his damp neck. "Come on, boy. It's now or never."

Alice led him to Archie's open stable door. Somehow she managed to get Secret to stand.

"Come on, boy, easy now," Finn murmured as he tried to encourage Archie to walk forward, realising that Alice wanted Archie to follow Secret out. Alice placed a hand on Secret's chest and gently urged him to back into the stable so that Archie could see his friend. Secret whickered and Archie whinnied back: a small frightened sound. There was another crash, and Secret shot forward, knocking Alice sideways and clattering out of the open stable door. Archie reared, and backed up so violently he almost snapped his lead rope.

"He's not moving!" Finn cried, his teeth gritted.

Seconds felt like hours. A wave of determination hit Alice. Somehow she still had hold of Secret's lead rope. She gave a yell of fear as one of the rafters, a huge old beam, crashed down in the walkway. There was only just enough room to get past it, Alice realised in horror. They had to hurry.

"Steady, steady!" she cried, trying to keep the panic out of her voice, patting Secret, singing to him, just like she had when he had fallen into a ditch as a foal.

Secret rolled his eyes, his red nostrils flared, but he remained where he was. He whickered again to Archie and it seemed to bring the black pony to his senses. Hesitating, he stepped forward.

"Attaboy!" Finn said encouragingly as Archie reached the door.

The two ponies touched noses, and Alice could have sworn Secret was telling Archie to follow him.

"OK," Finn said grimly. "Let's get them out."

Nodding, Alice started the walk back into the open air, pulling her T-shirt up around her mouth as Finn had done. The walkway was thick with smoke. Archie and Finn were right behind them, and although Secret was snorting, poised to flee, he remained besides Alice.

Crash!

Another rafter fell, landing between Secret and Archie. Archie gave a squeal of fear as Secret shot forward, the lead rope shooting through Alice's hands. Then there was a scrabble of hooves on cobble and Archie scrambled through the tight space between Secret and the wall, bolting for freedom. Alice let go of Secret, and rolling his eyes wildly, Secret followed his friend out into the safety of the yard. There were just a few steps between Alice and freedom, but looking back she gave a cry of horror as she saw Finn was on the floor, by the fallen rafter.

She dashed back and crouched next to him as he struggled into a sitting position. His left eye was completely closed, his face streaming with blood. Alice knew she had to get him out. She summoned every last bit of her strength to haul Finn to his feet, hooking his arm over her shoulders and shouting at him to run as another burning rafter creaked above them. Limping and clutching each other, they just made it into the courtyard, desperately gulping in the clear air, as the main supporting beam crashed down right behind them, blocking off the walkway altogether.

"You idiots! You stupid, stupid idiots!"

Sasha limped across the yard as fast as she could, holding on to both Secret and Archie. Handing over the ropes to Alice, Sasha looked as though she might pick Finn up and shake him, but instead she wrapped her arms round him, hugging him tightly,

before drawing back in horror as she noticed his eye.

"Oh my goodness! I'll call an ambulance!"

"I'm OK," Finn mumbled, wiping the blood from his face.

Alice was relieved to see his left eye was now open, and that the cut above it didn't look too big.

Finn steadied himself. "I'll go and check on the other horses; they must have heard the noise." And before anyone could stop him he lurched off towards the paddocks.

With Alice clutching both ponies and Sasha unable to run, the two girls stood in the middle of the old yard, watching the flames grow higher, the orange glow reflected in the ponies' eyes.

Sasha turned to Alice, her eyes flashing. "Both of you, I've never known anything so stupid! What were you thinking?" she cried. Then she stopped and shook her head. "Finn would have gone in anyway," she said, putting a hand on Alice's arm. "He wouldn't have let anything happen to the ponies. Or you, Alice. Especially you."

There was a clatter of hooves as Finn cantered back, riding Horatio.

"Hope and Robin are gone!" he cried, coming to a halt.

"Gone?" Sasha said in horror. "What do you mean 'gone'? Have they escaped?"

Finn shook his head, wheeling his pony round. He had bare feet and blood was dripping down his face. "No," he said grimly. "I think I know exactly what's happened."

Before anyone could stop him, he was cantering down the long drive towards the road, where Alice could hear the distant wail of sirens.

"Come on!" Sasha cried, limping behind him as fast as she could with her injured ankle, grabbing a startled Archie from Alice. There was no way Secret

was going to be left behind so Alice had no choice but to follow as he pulled her along. Reaching the end of the drive, it took a minute to process the scene in front of them.

Finn and Horatio were in the lane, blocking a white horsebox. Alice gasped as she saw Marcus was the driver, and there in the passenger seat was the blond man who had visited the yard. Marcus was crouched over the wheel, glaring at Finn. The sirens were getting closer, and a fire engine was storming up the lane. It was followed by two police cars, so Marcus's horsebox was totally blocked in.

Alice felt like she was watching a movie, and she stepped aside with Secret as the police officers got out of their cars.

"They're mine – look at the passports!" Marcus was protesting loudly as he stepped out of the cab. "See, look!" he repeated. "That's my name!"

Sasha lunged at Marcus, her rage unmistakable. "Liar! I paid for them; you know I did!"

"I don't know about that," Marcus said smugly. "You can't argue with a legal document."

"It was you, wasn't it?" Finn said slowly, climbing down from Horatio. "You took the passports while Sash was in hospital. I didn't think even you would go that low, Marcus!"

"As if you can prove that," Marcus scoffed. "I was a business partner. I was allowed to take the passports!"

"You were *never* a business partner, and I *fired* you!"

Suddenly Alice remembered something. "You went to see Fergus's brother and asked him to transfer the paperwork into your name," she blurted out breathlessly. "Sasha didn't know about that, did she?"

At the mention of this potential fraud the police

looked very interested, and stepped towards Marcus, who scowled.

"Why didn't you just listen to me, Sasha?" he hissed. "You put everything into that stupid team, living on nothing when you are sitting on a fortune! Why bother with something so pointless as the Flying Fillies?"

"Finn was right, wasn't he?" Sasha said slowly. "You haven't been booking us any shows. Did any of the shows cancel, or was that your doing as well?"

"It didn't take much," Marcus said angrily. "A few phone calls. And you still refused to give up your pathetic dream, your rotten old yard and your weirdo brother," he added, glaring at Finn.

"So you set fire to the yard," Sasha said faintly, clamping a hand over her mouth.

"As if you can prove that." Marcus had lowered his voice, glancing at the police. "If you'd just broken away, Sasha, none of this would have happened!"

"Never," Sasha retorted, holding her head high. "The Flying Fillies was my parents' dream, and now it's mine. You're completely crazy if you thought you would have been able to stop us."

Putting an arm round Finn, Sasha turned her back on Marcus. "Come on, Finn," she said, her voice clear and strong. "Let's go home."

★

The police let Sasha and Finn escort the horses to the yard where the firefighters had almost finished putting out the flames. The hay had been reduced to a pile of blackened smouldering bales and everything in the tack room had been destroyed. Somehow the building had escaped major damage, apart from the internal wooden rafters. Alice shuddered at the sight of the huge beam lying in the walkway entrance. It must have weighed

tonnes, and could have killed them instantly.

"It's those thick stone walls," one of the firefighters said, surveying the scene. "If they'd been wooden, the whole lot would have gone. The rafters will need some work, but the walls are intact."

"Yes," said Sasha, and promptly burst into tears, causing the fireman to shuffle awkwardly.

Finn put his arm round his sister. "Come on, Sash."

Alice thought about all the beautiful things in the tack room, lost forever. She knew they couldn't afford to replace their missing gear. This surely meant the end for the Flying Fillies.

"Come on," Finn repeated, turning Sasha round, guiding her in the direction of the paddocks. She followed meekly, like a zombie. "Let's get the horses turned out."

Still clutching Secret's lead rope, Alice watched

as Finn and Sasha put Hope and Robin back in their field. Sasha gave Robin a hug, burying her face in his mane, before they all turned back to the yard.

They were interrupted by Josephine's horsebox roaring up the drive, her face horrified as she took in the scene before her. She jumped out of the cab, and ran straight over to Alice. Secret whickered when he saw Alice's mum, and Alice realised how pleased she was to see her. It was only just beginning to sink in how close they had been to disaster.

"Mum..." she began, before the lights from the fire engine began swimming with the lights in front of her eyes. Dropping Secret's lead rope, she collapsed in a heap at his pale feet.

★

Alice was aware of her mum's arms round her, and of Secret standing quietly by her side. Her

mum gently pushed Alice's sooty hair back from her face. "What happened?" she asked, her eyes full of concern.

"Secret, Archie... We had to save them," Alice muttered, and Josephine drew her in for a hug.

"They are precious," her mum agreed. "But, Alice, you are more precious than anything else in the world." She pressed her cheek against Alice's forehead. The only other time Alice had seen her mum like this was after her accident with Honey when she had stayed by her bed for three days straight. "I couldn't have coped, if anything had happened to you."

★

Sasha was sitting on an upturned bucket, her head in her hands.

"You're going to have to ring Dad now..." Finn sat on the ground as the paramedics cleaned up the cut above his eye. "You've got no choice."

"You're right," Sasha said wearily. "I'll ring him in the morning." She looked at the smoke-blackened building and started to cry again. "I'm sorry, Finn," she mumbled. "I tried my best."

Suddenly Sasha looked very young. Alice stood silently with the ponies as Finn tried to comfort his sister.

Chapter 18

Alice woke early the next morning after a restless night's sleep, playing over the previous evening's events in her mind. Before loading up their ponies, they had made sure Sasha was OK and that the team horses were safe in their field. Finn had been taken into hospital to check for concussion.

Secret and Archie were back home, and the emergency vet had been to check them both over.

Josephine had cancelled her plans for the next few days and had called Samantha to let her know about Archie. Samantha had immediately rushed over with bags of carrots for the ponies. Finding Finn's number in the kitchen Alice had plucked up the courage to text him.

How are you, Sasha and the ponies? It's Alice, by the way.

She deliberated for a long moment whether to add a kiss on the end, and decided not to. He replied a few minutes later.

Sore, but no concussion. The police have been round all morning. Can I come and see Archie later? I want to see if he's OK. X

Feeling a tiny flutter in her stomach as she noted the kiss at the end, Alice quickly replied.

Of course, he'd love to see you. X

And so would I, she thought, but she decided not to write that.

A PONY called SECRET

★

The atmosphere in the yard was sombre as Alice relayed the previous night's events to Samantha. Although the vet had given both Archie and Secret a clean bill of health he had advised that they should rest for a couple of days, particularly Archie, who was still quiet.

Their conversation was interrupted by the arrival of Finn and Sasha. Finn was obviously relieved to see Archie, and the black pony whickered in greeting. Finn's eye was already a vibrant shade of purple, but the wound had been neatly stitched.

"What's the latest?" Josephine asked, her voice kind. Sasha was still pale, her eyes bloodshot from crying, as Samantha put her arms round both siblings.

"Marcus has been arrested for theft, arson, fraud, you name it," Finn said grimly. "He stole the passports and transferred ownership of Robin

★
★
181
★

and Hope over to his name. The police found texts he'd sent to that guy, Nick, arranging to meet at the yard that night and set fire to the hay so they could take the ponies. I don't think he meant to hurt any of the animals – but he did deliberately start the fire."

"What an awful thing to do," Alice said, shaking her head. "But it explains where the passports went!" she realised, remembering Finn had been unable to find them.

Finn nodded. "Yes," he said grimly. "It gets worse though. When poor Sasha was in hospital Marcus actually rang all the shows and cancelled our displays!"

"Why?" Josephine sounded bewildered, as if unable to comprehend that someone could act that way.

"Because he was greedy," Sasha whispered. "He never loved me; all he loved was what I owned.

A PONY called SECRET

When I wouldn't give up the Flying Fillies, he tried to ruin it all. The fire was a last-ditch attempt to break us, and I guess it did. Marcus wanted to set fire to the stables so we'd be nowhere near the fields when they took the ponies, and the hay was an easy target. He knew our horses were out ... but he didn't know Secret and Archie were staying." She shuddered.

She gave Finn a sad smile. "Finn saw through Marcus, way before I did," she said regretfully. "I'm so sorry."

Finn shook his head. "It's OK," he said. "I just had a feeling from the start that he was up to no good."

"What will happen now?" Alice asked quietly.

"I guess that's it," Finn said, putting his head in his hands, as Sasha put her hand on his shoulder. "There's no way we can afford to keep the horses. How can we continue?" There was a long pause, and Alice noticed Finn's eyes were misty.

"We'll have to sell them, I suppose," Sasha said eventually, her voice breaking. "I did call Dad, but he didn't answer. I've left messages, but I'm not sure what else we can do."

★

A few days later Alice was grooming Secret in the stable yard. Secret turned his head to nibble her shirtsleeve gently and she smiled at him. There had been a change in their relationship since the fire. Secret had trusted her when she had really needed him to, and she'd trusted him.

Just then Samantha's four-by-four pulled up and she leapt out, a huge grin on her face. "Hi, Alice!" she called happily, before greeting each pony in their stable.

Samantha was accompanied by two identical girls. They were even dressed the same, in jods and T-shirts covered in sparkly horseshoes. Alice

waved at them, and the girls grinned back shyly.

"Alice, these are my girls, Claudia and Phoebe!" Samantha said excitedly. "They'll ride the ponies one day."

Alice smiled at the twins. "You're very lucky. Your mum has chosen some lovely ponies. Finn's been riding them really well."

"That's who we want to see!" Samantha cried. "Is he here?"

Alice shook her head, checking her watch. "Sasha's bringing him over in a bit," she said, and Samantha clapped her hands together.

"I've got something to ask him. I've been thinking about it for ages!" she said happily. And then, without pausing for breath, she told Alice she was planning a huge party for the twin's eighth birthday in a few weeks' time. "And we want the Flying Fillies to be the stars of the show!" she said, smiling.

"We can't," Finn frowned as Samantha told him about her idea later that afternoon. "I mean, we'd love to, but the team doesn't exist any more. The fire destroyed all our equipment and props."

"I know," Samantha said. "But let me help! I'll sort out new costumes and tack. I know it won't be the same, but I'll do my best! The girls are *so* excited; they've been talking about you ever since I showed them your videos." She paused for breath, her smile widening. "And I would make sure you are paid *very* well. I've been telling everyone about you at all the things I go to – charity lunches, parties, that sort of thing. They'd all love to see you!"

Alice noticed the tiniest glimmer of hope creeping into Finn's eyes. "Really?" he said, sounding apprehensive, and Samantha nodded.

"Absolutely!" she cried. "I know once they see

you, you'll be booked up for months. Just tell me what you need, and I'll get it." She winked at Alice. "Any excuse for shopping!"

Finn opened his mouth, and then closed it again, before his face fell, the hope fading.

"But we can't," he replied miserably. "Even though he was awful, Marcus *was* good at the riding bit. And Molly's got another job. It's just me and Sasha."

"What about me?" Fergus appeared from the side of the stable, grinning. "I can't do what Marcus did, but I was in the gymkhana team as a kid. I'd just need a big enough horse!"

The glimmer of hope reappeared very gradually in Finn's eyes. "So could you still vault and pick things up from the floor?" he asked slowly.

Fergus chuckled. "Maybe," he said. "With some practice." Then he smiled. "But really, it's you and your sister who are the stars. You do the fancy bits.

I'll just be in the background."

"OK," Finn said, a grin spreading across his face. "What about you, Alice?"

"Me?" Alice gaped at him and Finn laughed.

"Why not?" he said.

"You bet!" Alice practically jumped for joy. Then her heart sank. "No, wait … my mum," she mumbled. She knew her mum would never let her take part.

"Let me talk to her!" Samantha winked, and she sounded so confident Alice felt a tiny seed of hope building. If her mum *did* say yes, this would be the highlight of her summer!

"Great!" Finn smiled. "Who else?"

"What about me?" Shelley appeared from round the corner with a grin, and Finn clapped his hands.

"Perfect!"

Suddenly he was full of enthusiasm. They had two weeks until the twin's birthday party, and

with the showing season drawing to a close they had plenty of time to practise.

To everyone's surprise Alice's mum agreed that Alice *could* ride!

Her mum gave a small smile. "Sure. Why not? Finn's been a great asset to the business; I'm sure we can help him out in return. But you must wear your skullcap, and you must stay in the saddle at all times!" She looked pointedly at Finn as she spoke.

Hardly daring to believe it, Alice nodded and fell silent. She'd agree to anything, if it meant she could ride with the Flying Fillies!

Chapter 19

The very next day an ecstatic Samantha and Sasha went shopping for fabric. A dressmaker Samantha knew was going to create new costumes. Josephine had managed to borrow a beautiful side-saddle from one of her old show instructors. To top it all off, the ponies had new bridles ordered, bedecked with silver.

"Amazing!" Sasha grinned as she unloaded

the bags full of rainbow-coloured fabric from Samantha's car. "We're going to look a million times better than before!"

Sasha was starting to look like her old self again. Marcus had been released from questioning but a date for a court trial had been set as the forensics officially determined whether the fire had been started deliberately by a lit cigarette. *There's no way he can charm his way out of that one*, Alice thought, pleased justice was being done.

★

"That's it … easy … now extend!" Finn called from the side of the paddock at Rookham Manor, as Fergus, Alice and Shelley practised the show. Finn had put together a new display based on fairy tales. He and Sasha were carrying out the complicated stunts but Fergus, Alice and Shelley were still having to learn a complex routine made up of dressage moves. Alice and Shelley were riding the two matching Dales ponies, Jack and Jill.

There had only been one problem. Fergus didn't have a horse. The thoroughbred Marcus had ridden had gone lame after galloping on the hard ground during the fire. So everyone had been surprised all over again when Josephine offered the most unlikely of solutions.

"What about Lachlan?" she said over breakfast, flicking through *Horse and Hound*. "He's totally bombproof, and looks just right for the part."

Alice turned to stare at her mum. "Really?" she asked, not believing her ears. Lachlan was Josephine's most valuable and prized pony, and having owned him since he was a yearling she knew her mum was devoted to the sixteen-year-old Highland.

Josephine nodded. "Why not?" she said. "The old boy would love it. But then it's back to business, Alice. Remember he's not yet finished his showing

season; we've still got the Horse of the Year Show and Olympia. But on that subject, once he retires," her mum continued, her eyes sparkling, "we can really begin to concentrate on Secret. I think he'll do even better than Lily, in time."

Feeling guilty, Alice just nodded. She desperately wanted to tell her mum that it wouldn't be happening, but now wasn't the time. She vowed she would talk to her mum, as soon as the party was over.

★

Under Finn's instruction, Alice, Fergus and Shelley were starting to look like a proper team, cantering side by side in perfect sync, crossing each other in the centre of the arena and galloping down the long side.

"It'll look even better when you're all dressed up," Finn enthused as they stopped for a rest. He gazed around, deep in thought, before his face lit

193

up. "I've got it!" he said eagerly.

"Got what?" Alice said, taking a huge gulp from a water bottle. This sort of riding was thirsty work.

"How we can make it the best show ever!" Finn said. "What about bringing in Secret?"

Alice just looked at him. "Secret?" she said, wondering if he had totally lost the plot. Secret, the pony who had refused to trot in the ring, and who had escaped from both his ridden classes…?

Finn laughed. "Yes, Secret!" he repeated, explaining that Secret could play the part of a cunning red fox. With his colouring and delicate face he would be perfect.

Alice gulped. "But what do I have to do?"

"Just ride him across the arena in trot, nothing fancy," Finn said. "You can do it, Alice."

"Yes, go on, Alice!" Shelley grinned, and Alice agreed reluctantly.

"Remember the fire," Finn said quietly just to

her. "He trusts you; you just have to show him what you want."

★

So Secret became part of the show and Alice had to admit the practice had gone well. Ever since the fire she had felt more confident about handling the roan pony and had ridden him in the fields surrounding the yard without any mishaps. But taking part in the display was a whole new thing. Finn seemed sure she would be OK. She would just have to trust him, and Secret.

Samantha returned the afternoon before the party with the finished costumes. Sasha had a new cloak in a rainbow of coloured sequins, and Fergus looked very handsome in a white tunic. Alice and Shelley had matching outfits: red tunics studded with silver diamonds. They even had silver silks for their helmets. Finn was wearing a dark green cloak and his hat was decorated with peacock feathers.

"You're not in black!" Alice said in surprise.

"No need, now I'm not the villain." Finn chuckled, and then gave her such a big smile that she felt her tummy flip over several times.

There was huge excitement in the yard as the team ponies were given a bath, even Secret, with Finn's help. They were going to travel in Josephine's lorry to Samantha's house the next morning, so Finn, Sasha and the horses were staying over.

After supper Alice wandered down to the yard to say goodnight to Secret. "Big day tomorrow, sweetheart," she whispered in his ear and he stopped munching his hay and blew softly into her hair. "For both of us," she added after a pause, remembering her vow to talk to her mum about Secret's future after the display. She had to get tomorrow right, both for Finn, and for Secret.

★

★
★   ★

"Oh my…" Sasha stared around her as the lorry turned slowly into a drive flanked by automatic gates.

Alice had to agree. Samantha's house was like nothing she had ever seen before: a huge mansion bordered by neat striped lawns, a swimming pool and tennis courts. A field behind the house had been set up for the party, complete with a pink-and-white circus tent and a big roped area ready for the display.

Alice immediately noticed the brand-new stable block to the left of the house. *Lucky ponies!* she thought.

Samantha had proved herself to have a brilliant eye for a pony, as well as being really nice. Although Samantha hadn't mentioned it, Finn had told Alice that she'd replaced all of the burnt hay. And now, fingers crossed, she would help save the Flying Fillies.

Samantha rushed over, laughing, and gave them all a hug. "Hi! We're all so excited! Please, get the ponies settled in." She gestured towards the stables. "You're on after lunch. Is that OK?"

"Perfect," smiled Sasha.

It gave them an hour to get ready. The ponies were unloaded and looked around in interest as they were led into the waiting stables. Secret whinnied loudly and bounded down the ramp, and for a moment Alice wondered if it had been a good idea putting him in the team. But Finn gave her an encouraging smile, so she took a deep breath and steadied the handsome roan, letting him take in his new surroundings.

The next hour was a whirlwind of preparation. All the ponies had ribbons plaited into their tails, and Josephine had even allowed Sasha to apply a liberal sprinkling of glitter over Lachlan's coat, remarking mildly that she hoped it would wash off

in time for the Horse of the Year Show. Her mum was being very relaxed, Alice thought. Maybe, like Secret, a change of scene was good for her!

She patted her pony, who was wearing his new silver bridle. Secret looked fantastic. With furry ears attached to the bridle's headpiece, red ribbons plaited into his scarlet mane, and a furry rug under his saddle, he was perfect as a fox, a hint of mischief sparkling in his dark eyes. Alice fastened her chin strap as Sasha chivvied everyone along, and gave Finn a thumbs-up sign. She was ready!

Chapter 20

Alice gulped as she clocked the eager faces of the waiting children and their parents round the roped-off arena. There were so many of them! They all cheered as the team rode up. Alice patted Jill's neck, who flicked an ear back in response. The little Dales pony was used to crowds and didn't seem fazed at all. Shelley grinned as she sat mounted on Jack, the other Dales. Alice's mum was going to

wait at the side of the ring with Secret while Alice did her first bit of riding, and then she was going to swap ponies.

As the music for the display rang out around the arena Alice felt a shiver run down her spine. All those times watching the Flying Fillies, and now here she was, part of the team! Sasha cantered in first, her cloak flying behind her, Robin's mane full of silver glitter. They came to a square halt in the centre of the arena, before rearing higher and higher as Sasha waved at the crowd, who clapped in delight.

As Sasha performed a beautiful leg yield in canter to the side of the arena, Fergus, Shelley and Alice rode out. Fergus led on Lachlan, and Alice and Shelley followed closely behind, side by side. There was no way Alice could attempt what Molly did, but even so the ponies looked impressive, cantering perfectly in sync. They were so used to being ridden as a pair that they almost blended into one.

Alice and Shelley completed a serpentine together as Fergus cantered the opposite way. He grinned as they crossed paths, clearly enjoying himself almost as much as Lachlan! As Alice and Shelley reached the top of the arena, they peeled apart and asked for an extended canter down the opposite sides, the ponies' tails streaming behind them.

Finn entered the arena up the centre line as they did so, and the crowd gasped and cheered as he threw himself off the side of his white Highland, until he was almost upside down, before standing up on the pony's broad back in one swift movement. He and Sasha then entertained the watching children with all of their tricks. Sasha asked Robin to perform a beautiful pirouette, as she sat barely moving in her side-saddle, and

Finn thundered round the edge of the arena in a daredevil gallop, high-fiving the delighted children's hands as he leaned out sideways from his saddle. It was breathtaking.

Then it was Secret's turn in the limelight. He seemed to be enjoying the atmosphere, jigging slightly from side to side, ears pricked. Alice took hold of Secret's reins as her mum quickly legged her into the saddle.

The music changed and the crowd shifted, eager to see what was coming next. There was a ripple of laughter as the children spotted Secret's costume and red ears. Alice clucked gently and held her breath. If Secret planted himself now, the show would be ruined. She tried to think positive thoughts, hoping they would somehow communicate to Secret, remembering how he had walked by her side during the fire. Secret looked round at her, fluttering his pink eyelashes, and

Alice felt a spark of connection pass between them.

Taking a deep breath, she nudged Secret into a trot. As his stride grew longer, and his silken mane flew, Alice laughed in delight, until the watching crowd melted away and it was just her and Secret, dancing together in their own world. He felt like he had on the downs: alive, wild and beautiful.

She couldn't stop patting and hugging Secret as they reached the other riders, and was aware of Finn looking at her in a way he never had before. Warmth, pride, admiration? Either way, it was the best feeling in the world as she brought Secret to a perfect square halt. It was only a tiny step forward, but to Alice it meant everything. As she watched the rest of the display, her hand resting on Secret's neck, she felt better than she had in a long time.

★

"Amazing, thank you!" Sasha was ecstatic as

they exited the arena. The clapping and cheering continued for ages, prompting the team to do a lap of the arena in a sort of pony encore. Secret had flown around, to the delight of the crowd, and Finn and Sasha had received an extra loud cheer.

"I can't thank you enough," Sasha continued, wiping her eyes. "That was the best show we've ever done."

"And it wouldn't have been the same without you!" Finn said, reaching over and placing an arm round Alice's shoulders, making her jump, a jolt of electricity running through her. "Well done," he said just to her. "That was exactly what I meant."

Alice turned to him, wanting him to say more, not wanting the moment to end, when suddenly Finn let out a shout and ran off, leaving Alice staring into space.

"Dad!"

Sasha looked up, and gave a whoop of delight as she too rushed to the side of the arena.

The man standing at the entrance had the sort of worn, suntanned look of a man who has spent his life working outdoors. Sasha flung herself round his neck as Finn stood to the side, wiping his eyes. He had such a rare look of happiness that Alice tried to push aside the sudden feeling of panic that had swept over her. She was so pleased for Finn that his dad was back after everything he had gone through this summer, but she couldn't help but feel sad that a special moment had been cut short.

Cautiously leading Secret over, Alice wavered, wondering if Finn would say anything, or if she should just make her way back to the lorry. Finn grabbed her elbow. Once again she felt sparks of electricity run through her as they made contact.

"Alice, this is my dad," he said, pulling her into their group. She was still clutching Secret's reins,

and the little pony followed closely behind.

"I'm Angus. Pleased to meet you." Finn's dad shook Alice's hand firmly. He had the sort of accent that you couldn't pin down, and his hair and eyes were as dark as Finn's.

"New team member?" Angus continued, nodding at Alice. She shook her head mutely.

"No, Dad," Finn laughed. "We've got so much to catch up on! Alice was helping us out today. But how did you know we were here? How did you know to come back?"

Angus frowned. "I got your message, eventually. There was no signal in the mountains. I've been trying to get hold of you ever since. Don't you ever check your emails?"

Alice noticed a guilty look pass between Finn and Sasha. She knew how busy they had been over the last few days.

"Anyway," Angus continued, "I finally managed

to get hold of Molly and she told me about this big party you were doing, so I thought I'd surprise you."

"Well," Sasha said, "you definitely surprised us."

Alice heard the bitterness in Sasha's voice. Alice wondered if she felt angry that her dad hadn't been around, after the way the summer had turned out.

"How on earth did you land this gig?" Angus looked up at the big mansion. "Not our usual scene."

"Long story," Finn said. "We got it through Alice's mum; she's a showing producer. I've been riding and showing her ponies over summer. I got paid."

Angus gave a start. "Really?" He raised an eyebrow, his lip curled. "Don't you hate that sort of thing?"

Finn shrugged. "It's been OK, actually. They're nice ponies, Dad. I've enjoyed it."

"Well, if you say so." Angus didn't look impressed at all. "But, Finn, you won't have much time for that now. I need your help; there's a pony in Spain I'd like to bring back. It's a difficult one."

Finn fixed his dad with a level gaze. "You know I'll help you," he said in a neutral tone, "but I like riding the show ponies."

Alice looked down, realising Finn still had hold of her elbow. It was as though Angus had forgotten all about her.

"Well now," he said, raising an eyebrow, "I'd better meet this wonderful showing producer who has turned you to the dark side."

"We've met before, Angus."

Josephine had appeared behind the group. There was something about her tone that made Alice's blood run cold, and she felt Finn tighten his grip on her arm.

"Josie," Angus said, slowly turning round.

"How are you?"

Alice looked at her mum, who had her arms folded across her chest. The tension between her and Finn's dad was thick in the air.

"You *know* Josephine?" Finn looked at his dad questioningly as Alice held her breath.

"We were both on a young riders' team, back when I was showjumping," Angus said – studying Josephine with a blank expression. "I lived up in Yorkshire at the time, long before we moved to Granny's house and you were born, Finn. Sasha was just a baby. It was *years* ago."

"It might have been years," Josephine said with a knife edge to her voice, "but it feels like yesterday to me. Remember Master Blue?"

Alice gave a start. Blue was the horse her mum had owned before Alice was born. He was buried up in the top paddock. Her mum rarely mentioned him.

"How could I forget?" Angus said, looking away for a moment. His voice was steady, but Alice detected the tiniest hint of something. Regret?

Josephine looked as though she might say something else, but stopped herself. "Come on, Alice." Her voice was ice cold.

There were so many questions hanging in the air. Finn glanced at Alice, shrugging his shoulders, before his dad swept him and Sasha away. Angus glanced back, just as Alice did and, for the briefest of seconds, their eyes met. Angus's expression was totally unreadable.

★

The party continued happily around them and with the ponies settled in Samantha's stables the riders mingled with Samantha's guests. Finn and Sasha were surrounded by people, all wanting to know more about them, and Alice didn't see much of them at all. Samantha was thrilled that the

★
★
★

Fillies were such a hit! But to Alice it seemed like Finn was slipping away, and there was no chance to talk to him about what was going on between her mum and his dad.

"It was brilliant! Everyone loved it!" Samantha said happily, linking arms with Alice and Shelley.

Alice smiled gratefully at her. She would be forever thankful to Samantha. Riding in the Flying Fillies had given her a small taste of what she could achieve with Secret. Once again she thought back to Honey, how they flew fearlessly across the country together. She now had hope that she could feel that again one day.

A short while later, as Alice was in the stables preparing Secret for the journey home, her mum joined her. "I'm proud of you," she said with a small smile.

Alice looked up in surprise. "Thanks, Mum." Compliments from Josephine were rare! Alice

decided to seize the moment. "Mum, what happened with Finn's dad?"

There was deathly silence before her mum answered.

"I don't want to go into it now." Josephine's voice was quiet. "Let me be clear though. I like Finn, really I do, but if I'd realised who his father was, there's no way I would have employed him."

"That's so unfair!" cried Alice. "You can't take it out on Finn. Whatever you and his dad fell out about, surely it's all in the past now?"

Pain flashed across her mum's face, and Alice felt a stab of guilt.

"Alice," her mum said in a steady voice, "you love Secret, don't you?" Alice nodded. "Well, believe me when I say I loved Blue just as much. And I'll never forget what happened to him."

Alice was really confused. Angus had said Sasha was a baby when he and her mum had been on a team together up north, and Sasha was twenty-three. Alice knew Blue had died just before she had been born, so at least ten years after Angus and Josie had ridden together. So what had happened with Angus and Blue years before he died? It was a mystery. She opened her mouth to ask more, and then shut it again as her mum held her hand up, signalling that the conversation was over.

"Back to Secret," her mum said briskly, "I know he's not been easy. If you can get him going like he did today in the show ring, he'll be unstoppable, just like Lily."

"Actually, Mum, I've been thinking." Alice took a deep breath. "Secret's just not cut out for the show ring, and I don't want to make him do it," she said, standing tall. "He doesn't enjoy it, and I know he would only get worse. He's been trying to tell me for ages, but I've only just realised."

Josephine raised an eyebrow. "Are you sure it's

not *you* giving up because it's tricky at times?" she said, and Alice shook her head firmly.

"No. No, it's not. Just give me a chance to find something else that makes him happy."

"Don't you think that's a bit of a waste?" Josephine continued, clearly not convinced.

"No," Alice repeated, firmly. "I'll ride other ponies for you in the ring, but not Secret."

Josephine sighed. "Very well," she said. "I can't stop you. He's your pony. But I think he could go to the very top if you persevere."

"That's where you're wrong, Mum," Alice said. It was *so* important that her mum understood what she was saying, for Secret's sake. "He wasn't happy in the ring, and neither was I. He doesn't have the right spirit for showing – I know that." She looked straight at her mum. "I know that because nor do I. I need to find something that makes us both feel alive. That we both love."

Chapter 21

A week passed and Alice hadn't seen Finn since the party, much to her disappointment. Her mum hadn't said anything about Finn or Angus either, and had been so busy in her office, planning the new season, that Alice hadn't been able to ask her anything. She tried to look up Master Blue online one evening, but although there were loads of entries dedicated to her mum's showing results,

she couldn't find anything else. And all Fergus knew was that Blue had been put to sleep at home.

★

A few days later, as Alice was cleaning tack in the last of the early-autumn sunshine, a familiar battered Land Rover trundled up the drive, Sasha at the wheel and Finn in the passenger seat. Alice felt her heart skip a beat and rushed over to say hello. Sasha immediately made a beeline for Fergus, giving Alice a quick wave.

"Hi, Alice," Finn said. "Is your mum about?"

Alice shook her head. "No. She's out at a meeting."

"OK." Finn sounded relieved. "I just wanted to see you."

"I thought you wouldn't be coming over any more." Alice didn't care about sounding eager. She had missed Finn so much!

Finn looked guilty. "I've been busy. There's been

a lot to sort out."

"It's just that your dad ... I mean ... he made it obvious he didn't want you to ride here." Alice scuffed the cobbles with her boots as they walked over to Secret's paddock, where the little roan was at the fence.

"Oh, he's *really* not a fan of showing," Finn said, grimacing. "He thinks it's totally pointless. But he had a long chat with Samantha, and he's agreed that I can continue to ride her ponies next season. Now he knows that Samantha helped us out after the fire, he feels we owe her something. Talking of showing, did you tell your mum about Secret?"

Alice nodded, smiling. "You were right: she wasn't as cross as I thought she would be. Has your dad said anything about how our parents knew each other, and what happened with my mum's horse?" she blurted out.

Finn shook his head. "Not a word. What about

your mum?"

Alice shrugged. "Nothing, other than it was something that happened about twenty years ago. She *really* doesn't like your dad though."

"Well, Dad doesn't want to talk about it, but I'm going to try to make him," Finn said firmly. "We've got a long journey over to Spain in the horsebox in a few weeks, so that's a good opportunity. But if you find anything out, would you text me?"

"Spain?" Alice cried in dismay. "You're going with him? For good?"

Finn shook his head, giving a small smile. "No, just over half-term. Once Dad told me about this pony, I knew I needed to help."

Alice frowned. She was sure that the Horse of the Year Show fell at half-term. Was Finn going to miss it after qualifying her mum's ponies? She would be furious!

There was a pause before Finn continued. "Now

Dad's back, we want to get the Flying Fillies up and running again, and make it better than ever. The party got us some more bookings. Molly has agreed to come back, and we're going to advertise for a fourth rider. And you'll have to come and meet the Spanish pony, if we manage to get her," he added.

Alice tried to look pleased. Things were working out for the siblings after their awful summer. But she felt Finn slipping away from her again. Spain … the Flying Fillies … his dad… Would he ever have time to come and see her and Secret?

"That's great!" she said, trying to look happy, and Finn smiled.

"Isn't it? But, Alice…"

Alice turned back to Finn. "Yes?"

"I'm looking forward to seeing what you and Secret are capable of," he said, reaching over and giving the little roan a pat. "I have a feeling that

together you'll be something quite extraordinary."

Alice leaned on the gate next to him and they watched Secret graze. The red pony who had brought their two worlds together by crashing through a showground. Secret gave a snort as if in agreement, and Alice laughed.

"What's so funny?" Finn asked.

"It's just strange, how things work out," Alice said, too embarrassed to tell him the real reason – that she was grateful to Secret for bringing Finn into their lives. But Finn smiled, as if he understood.

Slipping through the gate, Alice placed her arms around Secret. It would be autumn soon, and Secret's sixth birthday. Alice finally felt free to find her own path with her pony. She hoped Finn would be by her side... But, no matter what challenges lay ahead, she knew she would face them with Secret, her amazing, one-of-a-kind pony.

Acknowledgements

Thank you to the wonderful team at Nosy Crow, in particular Kirsty for all her expert help and guidance and Nic for her amazing design skills and for producing the most beautiful covers, which are exactly as I'd imagined them to be. A huge thank you to my lovely editor Sarah who totally 'got' Finn and Alice from the start and has been amazing to work with. And thanks to the whole team at Nosy Crow who support the books so brilliantly from start to finish!

Thanks must also go to our wonderful family friend Sandy. We chat for hours as we ride together and her wealth of equestrian knowledge has been invaluable.

Special thanks to Jolie Darton, owner of Butler – our beautiful cover star. Jolie made sure Butler looked like a superstar, ready to have his photographs taken by the very talented photographer Matthew Bishop. Matthew captured Butler's personality in every shot, making him the perfect 'Secret!'.

Finally, writing pony books really is the best job in the world and I must thank my husband Clive who supports me every step of the way. And of course my daughter Lara, who keeps me smiling and whose love for ponies mirrors my own.